I rose slowly to consciousness...

At first there was nothing but the sense of being in a bed. I did not dare open my eyes, for when I did, would I find myself again in a hospital?

"Are you awake, ma'am?" The voice was soft but insistent. "Try to wake up."

My eyes flew open and the world reeled before me. I saw an elegant room that was not, could never be, a hospital room.

"Where am I?" I whispered.

A middle-aged woman in a nurse's uniform looked down at me strangely. "Why, you're at home, ma'am. In your own bedroom."

There was a rap on the door, and before the nurse could cross the room it opened to reveal André Tate, the husband of Roma, the woman I had watched die. He advanced toward the bed, this man who had such a violent effect on me; who was, I was convinced, the cause of Roma's death. Panic, sheer panic, seized me.

"Well," he said, a light sardonic smile playing about his lips, "and how is Roma this morning?"

THE SATYR RING

ALISON QUINN

Harlequin Books

TORONTO • NEW YORK • LONDON
AMSTERDAM • PARIS • SYDNEY • HAMBURG
STOCKHOLM • ATHENS • TOKYO • MILAN

Published July 1983
ISBN 0-373-32001-9

Printed in Canada

CHAPTER ONE

SOMETIMES, EVEN NOW if I look down at the ring, a terrifying wave of loneliness sweeps through me. It happens mostly when a wild storm is brewing and I can hear the ocean roaring in the distance—or later, when the rains come flooding against the windows. Then it seems to me that I am thrown back to a time when I was alone in the world, the ring itself my only possession, my only hope. And I sit, transfixed, remembering.

Remembering the day, many years ago, when I first saw André Tate. Standing there in the hall of the Ellis Hospital, holding in my hands a bundle of his dead wife's personal belongings, I saw him through the glass-top door.

He was tall, toweringly tall, and handsome in a gloomy way—like a thundercloud about to burst. He was extremely thin, with hollow cheeks and thick, dark curls that clustered about his brow and temples like a Greek god's. His skin was fair, almost ashen, and his eyes were light too, but intense, piercing. When he glanced up, I saw that they were bright blue, full of ice and fire, hard like agate.

A kind of electric shock went through me, leaving me first hot, then cold. I could not go in there and face that man.

I turned abruptly and walked back down the hall. As I walked, I opened the bundle, took out a slim leather case, and slipped it into my pocket. Then I handed the bundle to a passing nurse to take to him and hurried away.

I had made my decision. Why the sight of André Tate, a stranger to me, had crystalized my feelings, I didn't know. I only knew that I would, I must, keep the promise I had made to his dying wife: I would go to America to see her grandfather and tell him I had been with her at the end. And then—this was important—I would stay in America. I would change my life.

In my mind it was already a *fait accompli*. But I began to perform my duties as a nurse's aide in the usual calm way. I took temperatures, blood pressures, plumped up pillows, helped incoming and outgoing patients all very methodically.

I didn't want anyone to guess that inside me my blood was racing. I was going away forever from this place where they watched over me so carefully, so solicitously.

I had been at the Ellis Hospital outside London for two years—since the end of the second great war, when I was brought in after a bombing raid. In the beginning they had given me up for dead. But Dr. Peters persisted, working over me till life flickered back. And finally, after a long convalescence, with the world recovering exuberantly from the horrors of war, I recovered too and was eventually pronounced well.

Except for one thing. I could remember nothing of my past life. I had amnesia. The doctors concluded that it was retrograde amnesia, the kind that comes from shock. It could have resulted from the bombing itself or from some incident preceding it. Either way, they said, there was nothing they could do. There was no cure. It would have to be left to nature.

The greatest hope they gave me was that one day, with luck, my memory would return by itself. It would happen most likely in an orderly way, step by step, beginning with the events most remote in time.

Meanwhile, what was I to do? I was young—the staff judged me to be eighteen or nineteen—and there was a world out there that I had to become a part of again. But how? I was without friends or family anywhere, as far as I knew—alone in a way it is difficult for anyone to imagine. No one had reported me missing. I had no home but the hospital and no possessions but the clothes on my back and the ring that had been on my finger when they brought me in.

Yes, I had one torturous treasure from the past: my satyr ring.

It was not a particularly comforting thing, this ring. It was huge, with a heavy yellow gold band. On the inside of the band were etched two entwined snakes that resembled a double *S*, and because of this, and the fact that they had found no other identification, they had named me Sara Smith.

The mounting on this ring was shaped like two hands, the fingers of which cupped around the stone. The stone itself, an emerald, was carved intaglio with a satyr's face, a face of such lifelike quality that more often than not, it frightened me. The head was thrown back in merriment, and the minute eyes gleamed mischievously. From the wide-open, mocking mouth, it seemed as though the creature were laughing at me. Completing its satanic appearance were two tiny horns in place of ears.

This ring was mine. But how? Where could I have acquired such a thing? Who could have put it on my finger?

I was fascinated—and frightened. This creature seemed alive. It seemed to be telling me something, yet not telling me. Any hint of recognition was always tan-

talizingly just out of reach. From the very beginning my
mind grasped at anything, at first hopefully, then frantically, until I thought I would go mad. At last Dr.
Peters, who had become my friend and was trying in
many ways to help me lead a more normal life, became
worried. He advised me to put the ring away—out of
sight—and to forget about it. He arranged for the
hospital to give me training in nursing so that I would
feel useful and could earn a little money.

In addition, during this time, he reintroduced me to a
world I could not remember: the world of theater and
music and art, and the world of books. He was a good
man, a good teacher, and I learned a great deal. Of
course, I grew to love him tenderly. But I wasn't
happy.

Perhaps it was ungrateful of me, but beneath the surface I was seething with restlessness. Once I had gained
my strength back, I felt too protected, too "watched
over." Sometimes, though I knew it was unreasonable,
the hospital felt like a prison, and Dr. Peters my jailer. I
wanted to escape.

But most of all I wanted to know who I was. And this
forever led my mind back to my ring. I had put it away
as Dr. Peters had advised, locked in a little black
Japanese box and buried deep in my dresser drawer,
where I couldn't see it and where the touch of it could
not burn my flesh. But, far from forgetting it, I became
obsessed with the idea that the ring held the secret of my
past—that if I could remember something about the
ring, I would remember all.

As soon as the ring was out of sight, I began to have
nightmares. I would see the fingers around the stone un-
wind and beckon to me. The head would seem to move,
still laughing, calling me. It was as though this satyr's
face had come to life and was trying to tell me some-

thing, to lead me somewhere. But where? What was I—a nameless girl without a past—to do but continue up and down the halls of the hospital, grateful for a refuge and the kind words of the aging doctor who had saved my life?

And then I met Roma Starr Tate, André Tate's wife.

CHAPTER TWO

IT WAS ON A MISTY RAINY EVENING late in March that we heard the squealing of brakes and the unmistakable sounds of a car crashing. It was very close, not half a block down the road, and the ambulance that went roaring out came back almost immediately. On the stretcher the attendants carried out was the sole occupant of the car, which had skidded into a tree and overturned.

The victim was a young woman, and they said at first that she was dead. But she was not. After careful examination the doctors detected some life and went to work.

I was handed a bundle of her clothes and other belongings to take care of: a beautiful soft purple wool suit and a lavender sweater; a string of pearls, miraculously unbroken; a watch, smashed to bits; a leather purse containing her wallet; and a flat leather case, which held an airline ticket, some American bills, and her passport. Mrs. André Tate, née Roma Starr. Born Boston, Massachusetts, U.S.A., 1925. Since this was 1946, that made her twenty-one years old and, of course, an American.

She lived through the night and the next night. On the morning of the second day, she opened her eyes, looked blankly ahead of her, then closed them again. She uttered no sound.

Of course, the hospital authorities had been desperately trying to contact her husband. They had located her London hotel, the Savoy, and found out that she had checked in only a few days ago. But her husband had left on the first day and had not returned. They had no idea where he was, nor who her friends might be. Even when they cabled her address in the United States, they received no answer. Their only hope, then, was to find out from the patient herself where her husband might be. But she did not respond to questions.

When the second day passed and the doctors walked out of her room shaking their heads, I asked if I might sit with her. She might begin to speak, I thought, and it would be wise to have someone with her constantly. They accepted my offer, and I began a vigil beside this lovely, comatose young woman.

I sat with her for the entire third day. Once in a while, she would open her eyes and stare at me, but she did not—perhaps could not—speak. But she began to improve physically. The doctors were quite pleased. They began to think that there was some hope she would live.

I continued to sit with her through the next day, hoping, praying for her. I was becoming attached to her. It seemed to me that there was some extraordinary similarity in our situations. She was about my own age. She had been brought in barely alive—yet she had survived. And she appeared to be alone in the world.

But there was another, more important thing. Ever since I had first glimpsed her lying in the bed, my emotions had been churning strangely. The fact was, although she may have been a year or two older than I, she looked like me. Even the nurses and doctors had remarked about it. I noticed it the first time I walked into the room. That smooth, pale face with an ever-so-slightly squared jawline, the rounded brow, the nose straight and a little too thin, with the nostrils tipping up a bit. Only the dramatic difference in hair color distinguished us. Hers was a glorious golden blond, while mine was dark, almost mahogany brown. If it hadn't been for that, I would surely have thought I was staring at myself.

It was an odd feeling. But it wasn't until she opened her eyes and stared straight ahead in a vacant unseeing way that my heart leaped. Her eyes were large and almond shaped and a deep, unusual emerald green. They were my eyes.

No one could have known what this did to me. As closely as we resembled each other, I knew that we could not be related. She was an American. She came from another part of the world, across an ocean I had never even seen. But just the same, it was as though I were in some way attached to her—as though I had found an instant bosom friend—for surely there had to be strong chords vibrating between two people who were such exact look-alikes.

Every moment I ached, prayed for her recovery. I longed to bring her back to consciousness, to speak to her, to get to know her.

But the third day wore on into late afternoon, and her condition didn't change. Every once in a while, she would open her eyes and stare blankly ahead, and if I spoke to her, I felt I was not penetrating her consciousness. Finally, another nurse came to relieve me so that I might go to dinner. Reluctantly I left. In the hall I met Dr. Peters and two other doctors, who were about to check in on the girl I now considered "my" patient. I reported that there had been no change all day.

Dr. Peters remarked that I looked tired and that I should go home and rest. But I was appalled.

"No," I said, "I can't. I want to sit with her. I'll come back as soon as I eat. Perhaps she'll need me."

He looked at me then, his own thin, tired face questioning my deep concern. He had been among the first to comment on our resemblance. Perhaps he understood some of my feelings.

"All right," he agreed at last, "but you must call one of us at once if she speaks."

I ate quickly, nervously, preoccupied with thoughts of Roma. Suppose, while I wasn't by her side, she should wake and want to talk? Or what if she should die? Hurriedly, I washed up and was about to return to her side, when an impulse came to me.

I ran out to the side of the hospital, where I knew some early roses were in bloom, and I quickly clipped three of them. I would bring Roma some flowers, some bright, sunshiny yellow roses to lift her heart. I went directly back to her room. The other nurse gladly tiptoed out as I entered.

It was dusk and very peaceful. The last faint rays of the sun streaked across her bed, and she looked wraith-like and a little unearthly. I moved across the room noiselessly and placed the three roses in a little glass on the table beside her bed. Then, as I turned to look at her, she opened her eyes. My heart began to beat fast, for I saw that blank expression had given way to comprehension. She looked at me first, then at the bright yellow roses.

I made an effort to sound cheerful. "Beautiful flowers," I said softly, "for a beautiful lady."

I thought I saw the faintest flicker of a smile. Perhaps now she would speak if I encouraged her.

"Roma," I began, putting my hand on hers and groping to say the right thing, but she spoke before me.

She said one word: "Baby." At least I thought that was what it was. Her voice was so weak, it was like a whisper.

"Do you have a baby?" I asked her gently, leaning

toward her. She made a small negative movement with her head. But she seemed to repeat the word afterward. I was about to speak again when she gained strength and asked me, "Who are you?"

"Sara," I said, "Sara Smith." And did not add, could not add at that moment, "That's just the name they gave me; I don't know who I am."

"Sara," she breathed, and continued to stare at me.

I fumbled to say something that might comfort her. "I know what you're going through. I know what it's like—"

Then her eyes clouded over for a moment, and I wondered if she was going to drop back. But she spoke.

"Am I going to die?"

A pain shot through me, and I put my hand up as if to protect her. "No!" I said. "The doctors say you're doing fine."

"Doctors don't know," she said. "I know."

I was seized with panic. I sat down beside her and took her hand in mine. "Roma," I said, "you have to *want* to live."

"Yes," she answered weakly, "that's true." And then she was silent.

I was torn. I knew I should run for a doctor. I had promised I would. But I couldn't move. I didn't want to leave her. I was afraid she might lapse back into the heavy silence of nothingness.

"Please," I said, pressing her hand to bring her back, "isn't there someone...weren't you traveling with someone...with your husband?"

After a minute she answered me. I had to lean close to her and strain to hear her words.

"We were...on a sort of honeymoon. But...he was thinking of...somebody else. Always looking for... somebody else."

I was shocked. No wonder she didn't care about living. What a detestable man! I didn't know what to say.

She continued to stare at me. She seemd to be looking to me for help, beseeching me with her eyes. But what could I do? What could I say?

Then I heard her mumbling, "Sybil, Sybil," and I knew that Sybil was the name of his "somebody else."

"Don't think about Sybil," I said, "don't think just now."

I waited, sharing her pain, patting her hand gently. It was a beautiful hand, white and soft with long elegant fingers, but there was no life in it, no fight. I suddenly pressed it between my own, wanting to imbue her with some spirit, some hope.

"Roma," I said, "you've got to try to live. And to tell me where we can find your husband. He's got to know what has happened to you."

But she shook her head. "He's too far away," she whispered, "always .too far away." And then she sank into silence and turned her head from me.

But after a minute she turned back, and a little life flickered into her eyes as she said, "Sybil, it's Sybil."

I was disappointed. I didn't want to hear about her husband's other woman. I wanted to know where he could be reached.

"Please," I said, "don't think about Sybil. I want to help you."

"Help me?" She sounded weak again.

"Yes. Tell me where I can find your husband—or any relative."

"Grandfather. Grandfather Benjamin. He'll know."

"Where is he? Where can we contact him?"

"Home."

"In America?" She nodded and I told her, "We've cabled there. There was no answer."

She looked puzzled. Then she lapsed again, closing her eyes.

I stood up. At least, I thought, she has spoken, told me something. We'll call the hotel again, track him down and make him...make him.... But I didn't know what we could make him do. Love her? Bring her back to life? Well, anyway, something. I would go now and tell the doctors. I was about to leave, when suddenly she revived.

"Don't go," she said, making a little gesture with her hand.

I stopped. "I only want the doctors to see you. I'll be right back."

"No!" She seemed to grow stronger. "Please...just you...stay."

I turned back, fearful. I didn't want to upset her. I knew the doctor would be around on his regular check soon anyway. I would wait. I sat down again.

"There," I said. "I'll sit with you if you promise to try to get well."

I watched her face relax. Her eyes closed again. We remained silent for a long while. But it was different from before. Now there was a conscious bond between us, a kind of special knowledge. She had spoken to me and to me alone. And I felt certain that if anyone could help her, I could.

I pulled a chair close to her and prepared to wait. It had grown dark, and the room was now lit by a tiny night light and by the great white light of the moon. It beamed in full across the bed, and I could see clearly her waxen face and her beautiful golden hair spread out on the pillow. A few wisps clung to the side of her face, and I gently pulled them away to make her more comfortable. Then I saw, close to her ear, a small red mark. At first I thought it was a cut overlooked by the doctors, but then I realized it was some kind of birthmark, like a small red bean, slightly raised. Carefully I replaced the hair. I wanted nothing to mar the beauty of this girl with whom I felt such kinship.

Minutes passed. I sat there, mesmerized by the quiet and the moon, feeling more and more akin to her until in my imagination I felt myself lying in her place, feeling her feelings and, in an unformed way, thinking her thoughts—suffering her pain, identifying with this girl whom I so resembled.

It was an engrossing sensation, and I was startled when Roma groaned a little and murmured in her sleep, "Sybil, Sybil—it's Sybil." She was having a nightmare.

How I hated that man, her husband and his Sybil! He must be cruel as well as unfaithful. I stood up, not sure whether to wake her. After a minute her eyelids flickered, and she opened her eyes and looked at me. She lifted her hand weakly in my direction, and I took hold of it. We remained so, holding hands in the moonlight, and it was as if we both were awakened to each other.

Finally she whispered, "Glad I found you. Stay... with me."

"Of course I'll stay with you—all night if you need me. You'll be stronger tomorrow."

She sighed and breathed, scarcely audibly, "Tomorrow...tomorrow...."

I leaned over and gently brushed a strand of hair from her brow. It felt hot and damp, and I was about to take her temperature again when she seemed to gather strength and to wake more completely. She turned fully toward me and opened her eyes wide and stared at me.

"Sara," she said, for the first time in a clear voice. "Is it...Sara?"

"Yes."

And then there was a long pause in which, ill as she was, she seemed to be studying me.

"What is it?" I said, leaning over close to her face. "What's the matter, Roma?"

Instead of answering me, she lifted her hand and touched my brow. When her delicate fingers felt the roughness of a scar near my right temple, she stopped and stared at me with questioning eyes.

"It's a scar," I said, "but it doesn't matter. I cover it with my hair." Then I pulled the hair down, smiling, trying to amuse her.

But she began to cry, quietly, weakly. At once I took her hand between both of mine and begged, "Roma, let me help you! What can I do for you?"

"My. . . purse," she said. "Please. . . get it."

"Of course. I'll be right back." And I raced down the hall, thinking, hoping there was something in it—perhaps an address—that we had overlooked.

When I asked at the desk for the key to her locker, I reported the fact that Roma was conscious now. I knew I had to do it, even though it meant that the doctors would soon come, and I would no longer have her to myself.

When I retured to her room, I placed the purse beside her and asked her what I could do for her.

"Open," she directed, and I opened it. Then she said, "Leather folder."

I fumbled for a second and then pulled out a long, thin leather case. She nodded and then said again, "Open."

I opened the folder, which had several sections. In one of them was her passport. In another was an airline ticket from London to Boston, and some American $20 bills. I flipped over these, questioning her when to stop.

"Next," she said. "Inside."

I turned over another section of the case and drew out a small clear color photo of an aging man. He was rather handsome in a rugged way, with thick iron-gray hair brushed back off his forehead. His eyes were blue, not green like hers. But there was a family resemblance—in the cheekbones, the nose.

I held it up for her to see, and she said, "Grandfather Benjamin," her eyes filling with tears.

"Where can we reach him?"

"Home."

"We've cabled your home. There was no answer. Is there anyone else?"

She shook her head a little. "Only Grandfather Benjamin will know. He's home...Maine. He'll... know."

"But we can't reach him."

"Go. You go...see him. Tell him...I sent you."

"But he's in America! How can I go?"

"Take this," she said, pushing the leather case toward me. "Promise me...if I...don't live. .take this and...go to him."

I stood still, believing for the first time that she was delirious. How could I go to America, and what would I tell her grandfather when I got there? That I had been with her when she died? That her husband had gone off with another woman named Sybil and that his granddaughter had died in the hospital alone?

"What shall I tell him?" I asked aloud.

"Tell him...tell him...." She sighed, almost too weak to go on, but then rallied enough to say, "Just—promise...you'll go."

Fighting back tears, I promised. I didn't know what else to do.

She seemed to collapse then. It was as though she had been hanging onto a thread and suddenly let go. I could almost feel the tension leaving her body, feel her sinking into a deep sleep.

It was very quiet. Night was closing in. The hospital stood hushed and a little ominous. I waited, fearful, in the heavy silence, knowing that the doctors would be coming momentarily. And yes—I heard their quiet footsteps. That seemed to rouse me and I took Roma's leather case and her purse and turned to go.

"I think she's sleeping again," I said as they entered, "but she woke up for a little while. She was able to speak to me."

Dr. Peters stood looking at me. "Did she say anything important?" he asked.

"I don't think so," I said. "She wanted to show me a picture of her grandfather."

They went over to the bed then, and I walked out of the room and down the hall, strangely dazed. I asked for the key to her locker in order to return her property but hesitated with the leather case in my hand. Should I keep it or put it back in her purse?

I was all too conscious of the promise I had made her. A foolish promise; a promise I couldn't keep—unless I kept her property.

But she was delirious. Tomorrow she would not remember what she had asked me. She would want her property back.

Finally I opened her purse and slipped the leather case back in. Then I quickly turned the key in the lock.

CHAPTER THREE

BUT IN THE MORNING on arriving at my post, I learned that Roma had died. An embolism, the doctors said.

My brief, ineluctable friendship was cut off. Roma Tate was no more. The loss was overwhelming. I felt bereft, unsteady. The world, which for a few days had seemed to hold some light for me, turned dark.

After the first shock and a siege of quiet weeping, I struggled to cope with my duties. But when I learned that André, her husband, had finally—and too late—come to the hospital, my heart turned into a knot of bitterness. I hated this man I had never seen, for I was convinced he had made her lose her will to live. He was "always too far away," she had said. Well, *she* was too far away now.

It was my sad duty to collect Roma's belongings and take them to the office where her husband waited. I tied up her lovely clothes, and then I picked up her purse. Inside was the leather case she had told me to take. And inside me, like a pointed knife, was the memory of the promise I had made to her. Would it be right for me to take the case and follow through? I hesitated, questioning myself.

In the end I left it where it was—in her purse. I knew that Roma had been feverish, perhaps delirious. It belonged by rights with her things. I would have to return them all to her husband.

I approached the office with my pitiful bundle—and

that was when I saw him through the window in the door: that man, that André Tate.

And something impelled me to take back Roma's leather case with her passport and airline ticket in it, and run.

I didn't know why then, but the sight of him, a stranger to me, had made me do it. Perhaps it was destiny, fate—but I knew in one lightning second that I had to go to America.

I was aware enough to know that wiser heads than mine would try to prevent me from venturing out on my own. Certainly no one would approve of my taking another girl's passport and leaving the country. And yet, leaving the country, going somewhere where no one could reach me, was probably the only way I could really be free. I would leave quietly, with no questions asked or answered, and no goodbyes.

And it seemed to me that that was what my ring had been urging on me all along. Get out. Live. Take a giant step.

Roma had put the wherewithal within my grasp. It was up to me to take it. I would go. Run. Start over again. And that meant that I would not reveal to anyone that I had amnesia. I would try to live as though I were like everyone else. And I had enough confidence now to believe that the things I should know would come to me. I believed I could take care of myself.

Consequently, with great restraint, I continued to work through the day, knowing that if I left on the following day, which was my day off, nobody would miss me until it was too late.

That night I wrote a note to Dr. Peters. It said:

Dear Dr. Peters,
    You must forgive me for what I am doing. I can't explain it or excuse it, except that I feel that it is

what I must do. I must "find" myself and my life in my own way, and so I am leaving you and the hospital. I have a little money and will be safe enough. And I really do have a pretty good head on my shoulders.

I have concluded it is the future I must think of and not the empty past. Thank you for all you have done for me, including saving my life. Now I must do something with that life. I will write in a little while when I have

Here I hesitated. When I have what? I asked myself. Secured a place for myself in America? Or found out who I am? Or discovered the secret of my ring? In the end I wrote simply:

when I have settled. Goodbye. And please don't try to find me or bring me back. I will be too far away.

I signed "Love" because I did love him—as a daughter loves a father. Then I sealed the envelope and put it in my purse.

It was growing late. The nurse I roomed with was on the late shift, three to eleven P.M. I didn't want her to see me making any preparations. So quickly, before she might return, I took out the little black box with my ring in it. I looked around for something to put it in and, finding a paper bag, slipped the box into it; then I put in a change of underclothes, a pair of pajamas and my toothbrush. That would have to be it, along with the clothes I would have on my back.

The following morning, before my roommate awoke, I was out the door and on my way. The first thing I did was drop my letter to Dr. Peters in the post box. And, I must confess, the rest of the day is a kind of dream to me even yet.

I remember only vaguely that I entered some beauty salon near the airport and asked to have my hair dyed a golden blond. It took an interminable amount of time. And in my nervous state, I couldn't read any of the magazines the operator thrust before me, although I pretended to. I held a large dog-eared publication in my hand and stared ahead. I think it was the most difficult time of all, those two hours of inactivity. What was there to think about but the bizarre thing I was doing?

It was there, in that uncomfortable chair, that I faced the fact that Roma, in pressing her leather case into my hands, had surely not meant for me to use her passport. It was her airline ticket, clearly, that she had meant to give me. She could not have known that there was no way for me, a nameless girl, to obtain a passport. But without it I could never keep my promise. So, though I felt a certain guilt, I allowed that thought to assuage it. I would carry through—go to see her grandfather and justify my little crime. And after that I would start to build a new life. I would be free.

At last all the washing and the fussing, the cutting and the combing and the curling, was over, and the hairdresser, in a satisfied voice, commanded me to look in the mirror.

I stifled a gasp. For there, beyond a doubt, sat Roma. I, Sara Smith, had faded away, disappeared. Roma's hair had been a little shorter and thicker than mine, but now, with my hair trimmed, colored, and brushed forward around my face, I had to shake myself to realize that I was not looking at that other individual to whom I had just said such a tragic goodbye.

I struggled to thank the hairdresser and to pay my bill

without showing too much agitation, although my hands were trembling uncontrollably.

From the beauty shop I went straight to the airport, where I remember having a confused conversation at the reservations desk as I tried to book a seat on the first plane out to Boston. There would be a two-hour wait, I was told.

I sat down in the waiting room, fidgeted for a while, then got up and found the ladies' room. I passed a full-length mirror and inadvertently looked at myself. I was wearing my best dress, a simple black wool, and my nicely tailored little tweed coat. I carried a black purse to match my shoes, and on the back of my head was perched a black felt pillbox. For all my inner agitation and my wildly palpitating heart, I looked like any ordinary traveler...until I moved closer and looked at my face.

It was white and frozen with anxiety. My eyes had turned black and seemed to have grown to twice their size. And then there was my hair. It confronted me in all its newfound glory, startling me all over again.

Hurriedly, I left the ladies' room. On my way back, I passed a shop displaying a variety of suitcases in the window. I stopped and bought a small canvas flight bag, large enough to hold my few things and my precious black box. Then I went back to the waiting area and sat down amid the swirling traffic of the world.

It was a thrilling experience for me, watching all the people pass, not truly seeing them but feeling the movement, the flow, of humanity. I was both exhilarated and terrified; in a daze and yet terribly aware. I had no regrets about what I was doing. It was, in a way, as though I had been destined to do this, as though I were seeing a purpose to my life emerge at last.

And yet when the call came for my plane, I was not at

all sure that I could make my legs carry me through the gates and up the ramp. I was in a state of bewildered euphoria, I suppose, and so, like a somnambulist I followed the crowd and finally found myself seated in the plane. I huddled against the window, praying that no one would sit beside me.

Luckily, by the time I felt the plane's final, awesome thrust into the air, no one had. It seemed as if the aircraft was half-empty, though I did not actually look to see. Instead I closed my eyes, wishing I could sleep my way across the Atlantic. I thought of taking a sleeping pill (I had one in my purse), but I had a sudden fear of being too groggy when we landed. I didn't want that. I wanted to be in control of myself. Wasn't that one of my objectives in setting out alone?

I sat with my eyes closed for what seemed like hours. Finally I had to speak to the stewardess; I was given dinner and then began to eat it. I found I was very hungry. The beef and potatoes, the coffee and the cream pie gave me strength, a burst of energy. I began to try to plan what I would do when we landed. I decided that no matter what the time, the best thing to do would be to find a taxi and ask the driver to take me to the nearest hotel. The following day, somehow, I would find my way to Roma's grandfather in Ogonquit, Maine, and tell him she had wanted me to see him. Only after that would I face my future in America alone. There would be time to think. That was as far as I could plan.

The plane droned on. I grew drowsy and dropped off to sleep. When I awoke, the stewardess was touching my shoulder and telling me to fasten my seat belt. We were going to land.

I came up to reality as from a tremendous depth, carrying the memory of my dream up with me. Of course it was that same dream I had had so many times before. It began as usual with my ring, with those fingers unwinding, beckoning to me, then fading into a vaporous atmosphere until I found myself wandering through many empty rooms, all of them open to the sky. And I was calling, "Where are you? Where are you?" And then the rooms were changing into a craggy seacoast, and still I was calling. And then there was the noise, the incredible noise, followed by a raging storm with the rains and the wind all but drowning me out. And still I called and called, "Where are you? Where are you?"

Only this time something new melted into the scene: two impenetrable blue eyes stared at me. They grew larger and larger and bluer and bluer until in a kind of explosion I awoke fully and heard myself gasp.

The stewardess was still beside me, asking me if I was all right. I forced myself to answer yes and to feel for my seat belt and fasten it. I was still struggling to adjust my mind when I felt the descent and the wheels on the runway, and I heard the bustle of the passengers, far noisier than before. They were rising, talking, leaving. I would have to leave, too. The moment had come.

At last I rose. My legs wobbled uncertainly. I gripped my flight bag in one hand, my purse in the other and resolved to quell the panic in my breast.

I stepped out into the aisle. At the same time a man left his seat across the way and we met, head on. I found myself staring at a pale, hollow-faced man with a shock of curly black hair and intense blue eyes—the same eyes I had just seen in my dream. The eyes of André Tate.

We stared at each other for a minute, and then I fainted, crumpling at his feet.

CHAPTER FOUR

I ROSE TO CONSCIOUSNESS SLOWLY, like a deep-sea diver coming up from the depths. At first there was nothing but the sense of awakening, of being alive and in a bed.

A bed? Startled, I felt the mattress, the smooth sheets. I didn't dare open my eyes. I lay there filled with fear and despair, for would I, when I did open them, find myself again in a hospital? Would I find that my fraud had been discovered? That everything I had carefully planned for myself had been blown to bits and that I was once again a helpless, nameless prisoner? And this time in a strange country. . . .

The very thought froze me, for now I was indeed alone. The walls of Ellis Hospital seemed like the walls of heaven. And the concern and care of Dr. Peters, which I had so resisted only a few days ago, now seemed like the protecting wings of an angel.

But finally I must have shown some signs of awakening, for after a little while I heard someone speak close to my bed.

"Are you awake, ma'am?"

The voice was soft but insistent. A hand gently touched my face. "Try to wake up, ma'am."

My eyes flew open, and the world once more reeled before me. I closed them immediately, for I had not been prepared for what I saw. I thought I must have been dreaming. I heard footsteps hurrying across the room. The owner of the voice had evidently run to tell someone that I had awakened.

Quickly, I opened my eyes again and saw what I hadn't believed at first glance: a most elegant room, decorated in a delicate shade of sea-foam blue. This was not, could never be, a hospital room. It was very large, and to my left were floor-to-ceiling French windows, draped in the sheerest, palest sea-foam fabric imaginable, which matched the walls. To my right, facing a huge flagstone fireplace, were two large oyster-white upholstered chairs with matching hassocks. Directly in front of me was a low, elaborately carved fruitwood dresser with one large antique candlestick on it, many small enamel figurines and tiny boxes made of gold and silver.

Bewildered, I took all this in until someone crossed the room with a tray in her hands.

"You're to drink this, ma'am, before anything else."

A lovely, soft-voiced middle-aged woman dressed in a nurse's uniform put the tray on the night table and smiled down at me. She had graying hair and mild blue eyes and a kindly look. I opened my mouth to say thank you as she helped to prop me up in bed, but no sound came out. She seemed to understand.

"There," she said, placing the tray over my lap, "don't try to talk till you've drunk this. You've been sleeping much too long. The doctor said you'd need something as soon as you woke. It's way past lunch, ma'am."

"Where am I?" I whispered, still dazed but unable to restrain my curiosity.

She looked at me strangely, with a little cock of her head.

"Why, you're home, ma'am. In your own bedroom." And then she poured some steaming tea into my cup and pressed me to drink it.

"You've been through a lot. Too much with your accident and all. Mr. Tate says you shouldn't have tried to make it home so soon. Here—put some sugar in your tea. It will give you energy." And she poured in a spoonful as I reached for my cup.

I gulped the hot liquid gratefully, knowing that I needed a boost for whatever lay ahead. Immediately I could feel the benefit of the strong stimulant, and I was grateful. As I drank she smoothed the coverlet a bit and then went over to the windows and drew back the curtains.

"A little sunshine will do you good." She smiled at me. "We're so glad you came back now, though. I don't think your grandfather can hold out much longer."

As she finished speaking, there was a light rap on the door, and before she could cross the room, the door opened and there stood Andre Tate.

My cup clanked into its saucer, and I was grateful that my trembling body was supported by the bed.

"Oh, I was just going to call you, Mr. Tate," the nurse was saying.

"That's all right, Emma." He cut her off quickly. "I think Mr. Starr needs you."

His voice was hollow, melancholy. He was dressed informally in a white sport shirt open at the neck and blue trousers that exactly matched his eyes.

"I'll go," the nurse said, crossing the room. At the door she added, "Shall I bring up something to eat?"

"Yes, please. Something solid and nourishing," he answered shortly and then waited till she closed the door.

We were alone, this man and I; this man who had

such a violent effect on me; this man whom Roma had loved and who was, I believed, the cause of her death.

He advanced toward the bed, and panic, sheer panic seized me. I clutched the covers to me and prayed for strength.

"Well," he said, a slight sardonic smile playing about his lips, "and how is Roma this morning? Feeling better?"

My throat was so parched, my body so weak with fright, that although I tried to speak, no sound came out.

Brazenly he removed the tray, sat on the edge of the bed, and stared at me from under his dark brows. He seemed not just to be looking at me but to be boring, penetrating, searching—not just the surface of my face but what lay deep beneath it, as if to tear from me the secrets of my soul.

It was this very thing, I think, that steeled me. I had to resist him, to fight him, to hold my own.

I mustered a little strength and whispered hoarsely, "Why did you bring me here?"

He raised his eyebrows in a supercilious manner. "Somebody had to take care of you."

My breath was coming short and quick. I felt like a trapped mouse facing a cat.

"When you came to at the airport, you were hysterical. So the doctor there gave you a sedative and I brought you...home." He said the word with a peculiar emphasis.

Finally I whispered, "You know this is not my home."

"Of course."

His eyes caught mine and he just sat there staring at me, not moving a muscle. Finally I pulled my eyes away, feeling weak and guilty. Then I heard myself say, "I'll go. Just give me a little time and I'll go."

Then suddenly leaning toward me, riveting his eyes on me and grasping my wrist he asked—no, demanded: "Good God, don't you know who I am?"

"Yes. Yes. You are...André Tate. You are—you were—Roma's husband."

He continued to stare at me for another minute, then he dropped my wrist and his eyes misted over, losing that frightening piercing glare. He got up then and turned to the long French windows and angrily pulled them open. Immediately a wild cold wind tore through the room. He stood there, his back to me, the curtains flaring and swirling about him while I went on frantically trying to explain.

"Roma told me about you. And I saw you through the glass in the door when you came to collect her things after she died."

And suddenly, remembering Roma and how she had suffered waiting for him, I became angry. And my anger gave me strength, made me brave.

"She called for you, waited for you. But you didn't come. All week long, she lived and she waited. I was her nurse. I know. I sat with her through the night. She talked to me, and I learned to love her...and...and to hate you."

He didn't move. He stood rigid, looking out the windows, his back to me still. My anger overflowed.

"I hated you because you didn't come to her. You were too far away, she said, always too far away. You let her die!"

He turned then and fairly shouted, "Be still! You don't know what you're talking about!"

And his face, as he approached my bed, was like a

thundercloud. ı was truly terrified and cowered against my pillows.

And then suddenly he was weeping. This great, fierce man, whom ı feared and hated, was weeping at my bedside. I had a glimpse of his tortured face before he buried it in his hands. And then the sobs came, and I was shaken by a jumbled mass of feelings that I was unprepared for.

I felt pain and sympathy, anger and tenderness: wonder, fear and perhaps a little triumph. Roma had suffered. Why not this man?

And through it all there was another feeling. A trembling feeling of attraction. I put my hand out toward him.

"André," ı whispered, then stopped, not knowing what else to say.

He began then to mumble the name, "Sybil, Sybil," and my heart hardened. I remembered that name. Roma had said it: "Sybil. It's Sybil."

At that moment there was a light knock on the door, and Emma, the nurse, returned, rolling a tea cart.

Without a word. André took flight. Emma bustled to close the windows, appalled that they should have been opened at all.

"What's the matter with him?" she complained. "Does he want you to catch cold, in your weakened condition? There!" She clamped the locks tight and then came to me, tucking the quilt in, propping my pillows.

"You must eat. Right away, while it's hot."

As she spoke, she lifted the tray from the night table, where André had placed it, and again set it over my knees. Then she lifted the silver covers from the dishes and put the dishes on the tray.

Ah! I realized at once that I was ravenous. There were steaming scrambled eggs, aromatic slices of bacon, hot rolls and coffee! No one had to coax me to eat! And I was glad when Emma told me she had to leave.

"You can buzz me if you need me," she explained. "I have to tend to your grandfather. Just eat and rest. You'll be better soon." And then she was gone.

I was alone. For the first time since waking, I was alone. I knew this was the time for me to think. But I couldn't. I seemed immobilized.

First I had to eat. And I did, quickly, voraciously, as though I hadn't seen food in days. And it was like a miracle. As I swallowed the hot nourishing food, I seemed to come back to life. Real life. I had so much to do, so much to think out.

As soon as I gulped my last drop of coffee, I pushed the tray away and jumped out of bed. I absolutely could not stay in it any longer. After all, *I* was not recuperating from anything but a kind of shock. And already I felt myself overcoming that. I was, in fact, exhilarated.

Yes, that was the word. Still a little dazed, of course, by the events into which I had propelled myself, but exhilarated. I had got myself out! I was away from the hospital and its protecting walls and, yes, eyes. Here, no one would know I had amnesia. I would never tell anyone. I would be free to work my life out as others did. I was beginning to taste the sweet thrill of freedom.

Of course, I would have to speak to Benjamin Starr and tell him I had been with Roma at the end, that I had learned to love her and that she had wanted me to come to him. It was, after all, the only justification for what I had done.

But after that I would quietly pick up my belongings and leave this place and find a way to begin my life. I felt my heart thumping, and my bare toes gripped the carpet in the beautiful room that had belonged to the real Roma. For just a minute I reeled and slipped back into the role of a frightened little girl. Everything had happened so fast, so strangely, that it was difficult to believe. I would have to strive for balance, for calm.

I pressed my hands to my temples and closed my eyes for a minute. It was going to take a great deal of will-power, I realized, to keep my balance. Already, in these few minutes, I had vacillated between heady exhilaration and fright. I would have to learn to deal just with what was, with what I had made happen.

I opened my eyes. The room around me was so elegant! No wonder it was difficult for me, who could remember nothing but a bare hospital room, to believe that it was real and that I was actually standing in it. I put out my hand and touched the back of one of the white brocaded chairs. Yes, it was real. Real and gorgeous. I would have to leave it very shortly. Why not try, for a moment, to enjoy it?

I moved softly across the thick white carpet toward a mirror, which was perched atop the chest of drawers. In it I saw a wisp of a figure in a long white gown, with hair of burnished gold. Was that I? Or was it a ghost, the ghost of Roma Starr? I moved closer, peering into the mirror. The only feature I recognized was the way one persistent curl fell over my right eyebrow. Even though it was a different color now, I was glad of it—glad because it was my own. My identification, in a way.

And all at once I smiled at my strange reflection, and that involuntary smile released the awful tension in me and replaced it with a kind of acceptance.

Suddenly I was cold. Here I stood with neither robe nor slippers. And I felt rather scandalous in my filmy white gown—I, who was used only to prim tailored pajamas.

There had to be a robe in the closet. But where was the closet? I looked around for a likely door but saw none—just the door that led to the hall. There was an open archway just to the right, however, and I turned and walked through that. It led to another room, long and narrow and walled almost to the ceiling with mirrors: a dressing room. On one side there was a washbasin and a long countertop, both in pale shell pink. The shelf above was arrayed with innumerable lightly tinted bottles—perfumes and atomizers and powder and makeup—all the things that beautiful women use but that were so strange to me. They glittered twice as much in the mirrors that reflected them from the opposite wall.

The back wall was mirrored from top to floor, but I could see lines that separated its panels, as well as tiny crystal knobs. I touched one and opened a door into a closet the likes of which I had never seen in my life.

Clothes! Exciting clothes, row after row. I stood bewildered, enchanted. In the first section were robes and nightgowns—silk, soft wool, velvet. And the colors! Dreamy pastels of blue, pink, ivory and peach; luscious deep tones of purple and green; even some wild-looking things of red and orange. I touched them, just barely running my hand over the outer edges, and then glanced beyond to the next section, where I could see the dresses. Here again were silks and wools in an array of colors. I looked at them in a daze. I walked on a little farther and pushed open the next mirrored door. Here were the suits and coats. I was fascinated and saddened too, thinking that all this was waiting here—and poor Roma would never come home to it.

I glanced down to see dozens of pairs of shoes lined up along the floor of the closet. And then suddenly I jumped back and gave a little cry. Something was moving in there! And, slinking out from among the shoes, was what seemed at first glance to be an enormous cat. But as he emerged, I saw that this was no ordinary domestic animal. He was more like a small leopard— tawny, with black stripes and spots. He stared at me with malevolent, glistening eyes.

We stood very still, eyeing each other—he, arrogant, fearless; me, terrified. He watched me intently, one paw frozen a fraction off the floor. I stared back with the uncanny feeling that if I moved an inch he would spring at me.

We had been standing like this for several moments, when I heard the door open and a voice say, "Good Lord! I forgot about Satan."

It was André. His entrance broke the tension between the animal and me. He came over and stood in front of me, shielding me. But he did not shoo the cat away, and I had the distinct feeling that this monster was the master of the situation.

"It's Satan—Roma's pet," he explained. "He's a devil of a wild beast."

We both stood there, not moving, while the creature continued to stare at me with an all-knowing gaze. He knows, I thought; he knows I'm not Roma and have no right to be here.

Finally, in his own good time, he made a slight hissing sound and sidestepped away, back in among the shoes. I sighed with relief. Even André breathed more freely.

"Sorry. I meant to warn you. That basket with the pillow in it is his bed. But he seems to like to hide in among the shoes."

"Is he a real wildcat?"

"Yes. He's a bobcat, straight out of the woods in back. She got him when he was a kitten. I think some boys killed his mother and were torturing him."

"And Roma rescued him?"

"I think so. Anyway, Roma and Satan were great pals. Inseparable."

"You mean—she could touch him?"

"She was the only one who could."

I shivered. "But he's so wild looking."

"He *is* wild "

"But why would she want such an animal?"

"She adored him—and the fact that nobody else could touch him. It made it more exciting. Don't you see?"

No, I didn't. Then a thought struck me. "What will happen to him now—now that she's not coming back?"

"We've got to keep him, of course. He'll slip in and out as he likes. Susan feeds him downstairs in the pantry. She puts the food out, and he knows where to get it. Just let him do what he wants. Stay out of his way."

I had every intention of staying out of his way, as much as possible. I shivered again. And suddenly I felt the warmth of a soft robe around my shoulders.

"Here," André was saying, "put this on. You're shivering. Sorry about the cold. I shouldn't have opened the windows."

I slipped into the wonderful cozy gold-colored robe, and as I walked past him into the bedroom, I felt myself blushing. Here I was in a strange house, not even dressed, with a strange man handing me a robe. He must have read my mind. He smiled for the first time.

"It's all right. We're supposed to be married, you know."

My blush deepened. I really was an innocent. And very modest. Only my bizarre situation had prevented me from feeling this before.

"Sit down," he said, "we have to talk."

I sat, pulling the soft folds of the gold robe about my

legs. He drew up one of the beautiful matching white hassocks and sat facing me.

Before he could speak and before I lost my courage, I said, "I'm sorry—about everything. I'll go as soon as I can. And I'll give back Roma's passport and, in time, I'll pay for the airline ticket."

He seemed not to be listening. "I suppose you don't remember what happened last night."

"Well. . . I remember I fainted. I'm sorry—"

"Don't be so sorry for everything," he interrupted impatiently. "You were doing a pretty risky thing. That's why you fainted."

That silenced me.

"We thought you were never going to come to. When you finally did, you were so hysterical, the airport doctor had to give you a sedative. He wanted to have you taken to a hospital, but I told him I was your husband and could have you home in an hour and attended by our own doctor. Meanwhile, I managed to have our bags and passports cleared. You were lucky I was there to handle things for you."

I gulped back tears of humiliation. "I. . . I've put you to a lot of trouble. And I'm sorry. I can't help it, I *am* sorry."

"Now don't cry," he said sharply. "I have to tell you the rest of it, and we don't have much time."

"Don't bother," I said, stung by his tone. "I don't care about it. I just want to leave. Now, if you will please go—" I stood up "—I would like to dress."

"Sit down," he ordered. "For God's sake, sit down. You can't go. You *can't* go."

I sat, because my knees gave way. What did he mean. *You can't go?*

"Now that you're here," he said flatly, "I can't let you go. Not after what happened last night."

I thought I might faint again. I struggled with every
nerve in my body to be strong. Why couldn't he let me
go? Was he going to turn me in? Or have me deported?
What kind of man was this?

"Please," I begged, "let me go. I didn't mean any
harm to anyone. I never meant to pretend I was Roma. I
only wanted to get away—and to keep a promise.
Please, try to understand. Just let me go."

"Don't get hysterical. Be quiet and listen. If you
would let me finish, you would know why I can't let you
go."

And then, as I sat frozen in the chair, he told me what
had happened the night before.

He had had to carry me into the house, for I was still
under the influence of the sedative. Susan, the maid,
had answered the door and, seeing me in his arms, had
cried out, "Oh, Roma; you've brought Roma home!"

And André, with no time to explain, simply carried
me up the stairs to the bedroom. Before he knew what
Susan was doing, she had run to Benjamin's room,
where Emma, his nurse, was sitting with him, and announced that Roma was home. His doctor had been
visiting, and was just about to leave.

The effect on the old man was electrifying. He had
lain paralyzed from a severe stroke ever since hearing of
Roma's accident. It had struck him down instantly, and
he had been unable to speak or move his arms. But suddenly, at the news that Roma was home, he began to
overcome the paralysis somewhat. He struggled to move
his arms a little. He tried to sit up. He spoke—not very
well, of course, thick and mumbled. But just the same,
it was a miraculous change. He became uncontrollably
agitated and demanded through gestures and grunts to
see his granddaughter.

And so what else was there to do? André had carried

me in to see Benjamin, and I had half awakened, and there the two of us had wept and embraced and wept some more.

At that point I jumped up. "I don't believe it! I don't remember any of that!"

"Of course you don't. You hadn't really come to. But you were in a terrific state of hysteria all over again. The doctor had to give you another shot."

"But didn't you tell them that I wasn't Roma?"

"No, there was too much excitement Besides, they had never seen Roma. Emma, the nurse, is new and the doctor was Dr. Henly's young assistant."

"So you deliberately let them believe I was Roma."

"Yes." He said it carefully. And then with that little aggravating, cynical smile on his lips, he added, "A very touching homecoming it was."

"But it's all a lie!" I was frightened, angry. "I'm going to tell them right now. And then I'm leaving—"

He lost his smile. He stood in front of me.

"What you have to remember is that Benjamin has accepted you as Roma. He believes his granddaughter has come home to him."

"But you'll have to tell him it isn't true."

"I'll do no such thing. I won't be a party to killing the old man."

"But you must. I can't pretend to be Roma. It's wicked. It's deception."

"You didn't think of that when you took her passport."

"I didn't *take* her passport. She gave it to me."

"That's preposterous. Who do you think would believe such a thing? People don't give other people their passports."

Of course. I knew what he said was true. Roma hadn't thought she was giving me her passport, only her airline ticket. The passport had just been there, in the case. I hesitated. Then I said more quietly, "She wanted me to see her grandfather."

"Why would she want you to see her grandfather?"

"Because—I was with her at the end, I suppose."

"Well then, you can see him. Everything is settled."

"Yes. I'll see him and tell him the truth and go."

"I tell you, I won't let you. If you try, I'll turn you in. What you did was illegal, you know. You could be arrested."

"But...but...." Real panic was seizing me now. I could sense the iron in his will, which would not be bent. I could do nothing but stutter. He glared down at me.

"If you leave this house now or let him know you're not Roma, you will kill him. Are you willing to do that?"

His voice was hard, and it pierced me like a dagger. I suddenly felt as though I were bleeding. I sat down again, my hands to my heart as though to stanch the wound.

"I...I don't want to hurt anybody," I said at last, "least of all Roma's grandfather. But—"

"But you will. He won't survive another shock. Do you want to kill him?"

He rose and came around in back of me and touched my shoulders. And his terrible voice developed a soft velvety quality.

"Don't you think you owe the real Roma something? Don't you think you *ought* to help?"

"But...how can I do it? How can I pretend?"

He leaned over and lifted up my chin. "I'll help you. Just do as I say."

I bit my lip and couldn't look up at him. Suddenly I was ashamed of the thing I had done. I had followed a desperate impulse in order to be free of the hospital, to respond to the goading of my ring, to follow its beckoning hands. I had seized on the promise I had made to a dying and delirious woman as a way out. I had meant to visit her grandfather, not to deceive him. I had never meant to involve anyone, just to get out of a stifling impossible situation.

But here I was in a situation far worse. It seemed to prove that there is no escape once you start on the wrong path. I sat there bitterly regretting the ill-starred, stolen journey I had taken.

CHAPTER FIVE

BUT I WAS NOT TO BE ALLOWED time for regret. I was sitting in Roma's bedroom, facing a man who was determined that I should carry on a deception that, according to him, had come about quite naturally.

He began at once to explain to me the situation in the house. Benjamin Starr was the master of Starr Mansion, where his father and grandfather and great-grandfather had lived before him. He was the wealthy descendant of New England merchants.

He had been a sea captain in his youth and an active vigorous man up until his recent stroke. His only weakness had been in his eyes, which had failed him in the past years. His vision was now very dim.

Roma had been his only living relative, and they had been very close. No one ever spoke of Roma's mother, and André assumed that she was dead. Her father, too, was dead now. But he had married a second time. when Roma was twelve, and she had lived with her stepmother and the stepmother's son, James.

When Roma was sixteen, her father had died. Soon after that her stepmother had left, and James, her stepbrother, had gone off to college. Roma and her grandfather had been left alone, with Marie to take care of them.

"And who is Marie?" I asked, making an effort to speak. I had to make myself realize that all this was real.

"Marie is Benjamin's housekeeper. She's an old and

trusted friend. Benjamin looks on her as part of the family. She was here at Roma's birth, I understand, and Roma loved her like a mother."

"Then will she approve of what you want me to do—deceive Mr. Benjamin?"

"I think she might, for a little while, under the circumstances." He paused and then he added, "But we don't have to face that question yet."

"Why not?"

"Because she's in the hospital. She's quite old, and she collapsed a few days after Benjamin's stroke. There was a great deal of stress, and she couldn't stand it. The doctor ordered her to rest to prevent a heart attack."

"Does she know about Roma?"

"She knows that she had an accident, but not that she died. I was coming home to break it to them in person. I thought I might be able to cushion the shock."

"And now?"

"I *will* tell her, but it can wait a bit. And meanwhile, no one here need know."

I sat very still, even more frightened now, realizing that our grim little charade was to be a secret between us.

"Now," he went on, oblivious to what he was doing to me, "the only other people in the house are Emma, the nurse, who never knew Roma; Susan, the maid; and Harry, the handyman. None of them need concern us."

Suddenly I thought of a way out. "There's one thing you haven't covered—I have an English accent. I won't sound like Roma."

He brushed this aside. "Your accent is very slight—Benjamin will think you've acquired it in the two months you were over there. He knows Roma was a great mimic. And I'll teach you some of the expressions Roma used." Then, pleadingly, he added, "He will live only if he thinks he has Roma to live for. You can help him—or help to kill him."

He was imposing a responsibility on me. "I want to help him, of course, but—"

"Then do as I say. Trust me, please."

The pleading in his voice made me, for the moment, think of him instead of myself. It was I, this time, who stared at him.

Once again, I found myself feeling something other than hatred for this man. My hatred did not disappear, but it lessened. I had thought his treatment of Roma detestable, and I considered his proposition to be quite improper. And yet—there was this pain, this haunted look in his eyes. And now, his strong desire to save Benjamin, to shield him from a fatal shock. How could this be bad?

There was a long silence while I sat in the chair facing him, studying him. He had pulled his hassock up close, leaning his elbows on his knees and occasionally clasping and unclasping his long thin strong fingers. After a while he returned my stare.

I watched his expression change in those few minutes from steely cold to cloudy and yearning, to tragic. His blue eyes became dark tunnels of pain.

I forgot myself entirely then. Involuntarily I reached out my hand and touched his, the gesture of a woman to a suffering fellow creature.

And then in hushed tones he asked, "Tell me, why are you staring at me?"

I didn't know I was going to say it, but it came from somewhere inside me, from some deep place that spoke for me.

"I'm trying to decide," I said, "whether you are a very good man.. or a very wicked one."

He continued to stare at me, not moving a muscle,

until I began to be frightened again. It was impossible to
sustain such a penetrating look. I had to break the spell.

"André," I whispered.

And with the word I felt him move toward me. His
fingers tightened painfully around my arms, and he
pulled me close—so close that I felt his hard chest and
the fierce trembling of his body. I knew he was about
to kiss me, but suddenly, as though some force had
gripped him and pulled him back, he wrenched himself
away and rushed to the long windows. Pushing them
open, he stepped out onto the small balcony.

I followed him impulsively but stopped short, seeing
his back hunched over and his head in his hands, and
hearing muffled agonized sobs.

I stood there trying to reappraise this man. Had I
been wrong about him? Had he truly loved Roma? No
man, surely, could suffer like this and not have loved.

And what was this feeling he had for me, if not that I
reminded him of Roma? And what was my feeling for
him, that every time I encountered him I should be so
devastated in one way or another?

Suddenly I was aware that it was quiet. He had
stopped sobbing, and had straightened his shoulders. I
stepped out onto the balcony, full into the racing wind
that had already chilled the room.

I gasped. For a moment I forgot even André. I was
overwhelmed. For there, there before me, was my
craggy seacoast—the seacoast of my dreams. Only now
I wasn't frightened. I was thrilled to my bones. The
great waves rose and broke against ancient rocks, spray-
ing white mist, then rising and plunging again to rough,
wild, raging depths of darkest green.

Some unimagined vitality welled up in me, and I
gasped again and again, breathless with the wonder of
it. Finally I whispered, "This is *my* ocean!" Then I

mumbled a French phrase that I didn't even know that I knew: *"C'est mon pays."*

"What are you saying?" André's voice came to me as from a great distance. "Have you been here before?"

"Only in my dreams," I answered, still mesmerized by the sight of that ocean.

I stood there listening to the thunder against the rocks, to the cries of the gulls, feeling the wind through my hair, through my bones.

"But I suppose," I said at last, "all oceans are alike."

"No, there's nothing like the coast of Maine, the wild coast of Maine." He paused, before adding, "Except, perhaps, the sea at Cornwall, England."

He looked down at me as he said it, as though he expected some reply. As though he thought I might have known the coast of Cornwall, when all I really knew were the walls of the Ellis Hospital. Well, *he* would never know that.

He went on after a minute, "We're on a cliff here, as you can see. It's pretty rough, but beautiful. It's lonely here now and that's the way we like it best. In summer there are visitors, outsiders. It's a pleasant resort, closer in to town, that is. Out here we're very much alone...."

He drifted off and we stood there silent. It seemed natural when he put his arm around me. After all, I was shivering. For a few moments, all the troubles of the world were washed away.

And then, standing there, his voice as resonant as the wind, he said softly, almost like a priest, "You know, I've been waiting for you to tell me something. You still haven't told me that most important thing."

The vastness of the ocean before me made everything

seem insignificant and therefore excusable—even what I had done.

I answered easily, "What do you want to know? What haven't I told you?"

"Why did you take my wife's passport?"

"I didn't have one of my own. And Roma wanted me to come see her grandfather. I think she thought it would comfort him to see someone who had been with her at the end."

"Perhaps it will," he said.

"Perhaps. But that should have been *you*. You should have been with her—"

"Of course, but—"

"Yes, she told me. You were too far away—with your Sybil."

My bitterness against him welled up, rushed back through me like a flood. I pulled away from him.

"Will it help if I tell you that I didn't find her—where I went?"

"It's too late. Nothing will help now."

There was a silence and then a deep sigh from him.

"Perhaps it won't."

We stood for just a few more minutes, staring out over the magnificent sea, breathing the strong-scented air, each in our own private world.

Then suddenly, abruptly, he pulled me away from the balcony railing and into the bedroom again. He stopped to close the windows, and when he turned around, he was a changed man. It was the first time I had ever seen the melancholy look washed from his face. It was as though the dead embers I thought I saw in his eyes were suddenly lit by some new spark.

"Come," he said almost gaily, "we've wasted too much time. And you're freezing."

Then, before I could answer or protest, he said, "Put

on a warm sweater and skirt—there are plenty there. I've got to show you around the house, give you a tour.''

When I didn't move, he opened a few drawers in the bureau, then led me into the dressing room and opened the closet. ''There, there's everything you need. But hurry. I'll be back in ten minutes.''

And he was gone. I stood immobilized physically, but racing inside. He had infected me with his new excitement. And yet... and yet.... Finally I moved. Something in me just operated, did as I was told. I found Roma's sweaters. Such an array! In my wildest dreams I had never imagined myself choosing from such a wardrobe. And such colors!

Quickly, I chose the red. Why? Red had never been a color I had worn. Perhaps that was the very reason. Did it denote rebellion? Fire? Action? A new life?

I slipped into it, soft and warm. Then I looked at the skirts hanging in the closet. I found one to match, of course.

Once I'd put the skirt on, the mirrors all around me reflected a slight girl, very pale, almost frail looking, whose flame-colored outfit suddenly seemed to fill her with life. There was a new glow in her cheeks, even in her hair.

I was ''alive'' as I had never seen myself, but as I had imagined Roma would have looked when she was well and happy: skin glowing with an inner light, blond hair shining, curling gently around her smooth oval face, and eyes flickering with lights of green and gold.

The chameleon, I thought, as I stood staring. Already you are taking on her identity. Against your will—or *with* it?

By this time I was so confused, I didn't know. I had wanted to be master of my life, to control it; that had been the whole purpose of my escape. And yet here I was playing a cruel game, deceiving an old man.

Was it right? Could I go on with it?

I remembered André's threat to turn me in, to expose me. And more frightening than that, I thought of his eyes, his pained cavernous eyes. What was there about this man? Did I hate him? Perhaps I didn't.

But old Mr. Benjamin—was I doing what was right for him? Was it really necessary to deceive him?

And then, as I stood lost in thought, trying to answer all the unanswerable questions, I felt a presence.

I looked up over my shoulder—and there was the wildcat, Satan! What a fitting name!

He had crawled out of the closet and somehow managed to climb noiselessly onto the top of it, where it formed a kind of shelf. From there, high above my head, he was staring, unmoving, at me.

I felt as though some creature of the jungle had singled me out for his prey. Patiently, he sat and stared.

I began to tremble before this creature, who might, if he wished, jump down on me and claw me.

I was growing hot and weak. By the time André opened the bedroom door, I was ready to run. I would have to escape. He would have to let me. . . .

But before I could speak, he closed the door and said in a taut voice, "You've got to go to Benjamin. Now. At once."

We stood there; I, now in the center of the room in my flaming-red clothing, and André, his back against the door, the two of us like statues.

This was the moment then. Either I follow him or? . . . My whole body turned from hot to cold.

And then André sprang to life. "I said, you'll have to come. Benjamin is awake and he's calling for you."

I stood still, staring at him. I could feel my eyes growing wide with fear. When he moved a step closer and opened his mouth to speak, I exploded.

"No! No, no, no! I won't go in there! How do I know what you're up to? Why should you be doing this? You've forced me into doing something I don't think is right, something I never intended to do. You brought me here when I was unconscious, and now you think I'm trapped and I'll have to do what you say. But I won't! I won't! I can't. I've got to see somebody else. I've got to see a. . .a doctor. Somebody. I'm too alone. I'm at your mercy!. . .''

I was shouting, thoughts pouring out of me I didn't even know I had been thinking. But they seemed to make some sense as I spoke them—only not to André.

He took on as fierce and thunderous an expression as I had ever seen. Had I not been in such a white heat I would have cowered before it. As it was, I faced him, strengthened by my own fire.

"How do I know what you're up to?" I cried. "You're using me for something. What is it? Why did you bring me here? You didn't know Benjamin was stricken when you brought me here. Why did you do it? You knew I wasn't Roma then. You *knew* it. Why did you bring me here?"

Suddenly I stopped. The fact that he had let me go on uninterrupted had somewhat exhausted my fire. In the moment's silence he grabbed me by the shoulders and forced me to sit down on the edge of the bed.

"Listen," he said between his teeth, "be quiet and listen! Yes, I knew you weren't Roma. I had just finished taking care of her remains.

"But what do you think I should have done? Exposed you to the customs officials? Exposed you while you were lying in a faint? And leave you there for them to deal with? Would you rather I had done that?

"If you want to know, it was out of the kindness of my heart that I brought you here. And as you say, I didn't know that Benjamin was ill, and I didn't plan that he should take you for his granddaughter. But he did, and you are going to have to pay the price for your own deception.

"And while you're asking questions, I have a question for you. What did you intend to do when you got here? Could you have been planning to actually pass yourself off as Roma?"

That final thrust shot me to my feet again.

"How *can* you!" I breathed, almost choking on the words.

"Well," he raged, "what do I know of you and your intentions? Why shouldn't I turn you in?"

He was white with fury. As his anger mounted, mine subsided. Of course. There was no reason he shouldn't. I was caught in my own trap. My fire spent, I began to crumble.

"It's very strange," he went on, "the whole thing. But if I were you, I wouldn't be quite so quick to accuse other people. Your own position is too precarious. You could be under arrest now, you know, if it weren't for me. And whether you like it or not, the deception has already been perpetrated. Carrying it a little further might save an old man's life. Break the illusion at this moment, and you'll certainly kill him. Take your choice."

He seemed to toss the words at my feet as one would toss a gauntlet.

I turned away so that he couldn't see the tears gathering in my eyes again. I felt wretched, utterly wretched, and all mixed up.

After a minute he came up quietly behind me and turned me around to face him. I looked up and saw the same bewilderment in his eyes that I felt must be in my own.

We stared at each other, as if to find the answers to the questions we had asked. But there were no answers.

Instead he spoke in his practical voice. Another question: "Do you want to come, or not?"

I hesitated a moment. Then I said quietly, "I'll come."

CHAPTER SIX

IT SEEMS TO ME NOW that my life has been a series of traumatic episodes. And my meeting with Benjamin Starr was one of these. I was never quite the same after that momentous afternoon.

I was shaking inwardly as André stood waiting for me, and I knew I would have to do something to pull myself together. I hesitated a moment, then I walked past him into the dressing room.

The girl who faced me now in the mirrors seemed like a mirage, someone who wasn't really there. It surprised me a little to see a hand go up and smooth the golden hair. How ghostly this new light shade made me appear! My skin was blanched, so pale, I looked like a wraith who might disappear at any moment, consumed by the flame of my sweater.

Quickly, to try to bring some life back into me, I turned on the faucet and splashed the water on my face. At least the tingling sensation this produced was real. The blood came back to my face a little, and with a kind of relief, I patted it dry.

As I began to smooth my hair, André spoke to me quietly. "Brush your hair forward, in front of your ears."

I did as he bade me, changing my appearance at once.

"Yes," he said. "Now, by God, you look exactly like her. Don't forget. That's the way she always wore it Forward over her ears."

"My hair is trained to go the other way. I don't think it will stay this way."

"Then retrain it," he said. "You must. She never wore it brushed back."

A streak of rebellion ran through me. I hadn't bargained for this—to bury my own personality, my own way of doing things, even down to combing my hair. It was with the greatest of effort that I controlled myself.

I didn't answer him. I just stood up, and we both walked silently out of the room.

"This is your home," he said as he closed the door behind me. "Look around."

We stood in a wide hallway softly carpeted in a deep warm red. There were rooms on only one side, all along the right. On the opposite side was a banister overlooking the lower floor. I could see a large foyer below with a white fan-topped doorway in the center and rooms opening on either side. Before I could take in more, André drew my attention to the doors along the hallway.

"The bedrooms are all along here. Yours, as you see, is the first door at the top of the stairs. Your grandfather's is at the end of the hall, the corner room facing front and side. By the way," he added, "you call him Grandfather Benjamin. You love him very much, but you don't bend to his will. You are supposed to be like him, stubborn and willful."

I said nothing, listening in a kind of dream.

"There are two other bedrooms back there, beyond yours. And these rooms here, between yours and Benjamin's, are all unoccupied now."

"All?" I asked sharply. "Where do you sleep then?"

He looked down at me with faint amusement. "Well, you know Roma and I were married. We shared her room."

I felt myself blushing.

"But don't worry. I'm sleeping upstairs now, in my studio."

"Studio?"

"Yes. Didn't you know? I'm an artist, a painter."

"How would I know?"

He ignored the edge in my voice. "It gets pretty messy painting, and I need a skylight and space. So I work on the third floor. Up there through that door at the end of the hall. We'll pretend that I sleep there now because of your accident, until you recuperate."

We had reached Benjamin's room. André took my hand and stopped. With his other hand on the doorknob, he said, "You don't have to say much or stay very long. All he needs is to feel you there."

He pushed the door open and left me.

I realize now that before I entered Benjamin Starr's bedroom I was a thing adrift, like a cork bobbing in the sea. I was nothing but a bundle of nerves and longings— without a country, without a family, without a friend.

But as André closed the door behind me and I walked alone toward the old man's great four-poster mahogany bed, a feeling came over me of what the French call *déjà vu*: "I have been here before."

I hadn't been there, of course; not actually. But something deep within me was stirred to life. I saw a gaunt cadaverous face, eyes closed and sunken around the sockets, cheeks waxen and hollowed out, lips finely carved as in stone. And atop the high forehead was a great thick growth of iron-gray hair. Grandfather Benjamin lay still, his long arms and large-boned hands on top of the bedspread, his figure outlined beneath it, flat and wasted.

I was conscious of many pieces of heavy mahogany furniture: a highboy, a desk, a large table and a small one, two leather chairs, a bookcase, a fireplace.

This was a man's room, belonging to someone who had lived here many years, someone who had been somebody's father, somebody's grandfather.

For the first time since I woke up in Ellis Hospital, I felt what it was like to have a grandfather. I felt it not with my head, but with my heart. I could almost remember something.... The feeling hung there tenuously, agonizingly, all around me.

And then Benjamin Starr opened his eyes. He raised his arm an inch off the bed and strained his eyes, searching.

"Roma!" His lips hardly formed the sound, but I knew what it was that he was trying to say. "Roma." He sensed, rather than saw, the figure near his bed.

And then, without thinking at all about what would be right to do, I fell on the dear old man's chest and hugged him and kissed him. As I pressed my wet cheek to his, there seemed no need for words.

After a while I lifted my head, and I could see him struggling to move his lips. As I dried his tears with a handkerchief, he spoke with difficulty, thickly and haltingly.

"My...dear...my...Roma." My heart ached for him. I could see he was struggling to move his hands in order to touch me, and I helped him by placing my hand in his. His touch was cold, but in a way his large hands were comforting.

And then he struggled with what I thought was, "Are...you...all right...my dear?"

"Yes," I whispered, "I'm fine."

He seemed pleased at that. I saw a flicker of a smile. Then, after a long pause, he said, "I thought...I was...afraid...my darling."

The tears were flowing down his cheeks again, and I had trouble stopping mine. Then, with tremendous ef-

fort, he said, "Don't...go...away. Stay...with...
me."

"I'll stay," I said, "I won't go away. But you ought
to rest now. Don't try to talk. I'll just sit with you."

I felt a slight pressure on my hand, all that he could
muster, and I knew that he was very weak. I sat still,
watching the fine old face relax into an exhausted smile.
Perhaps a half hour passed as we sat in silence. Then the
door opened and Emma entered, followed closely by
André.

He gave me a questioning look while Emma glanced
at the clock and picked up a bottle of pills.

"It's time for his medicine, Mrs. Tate. I think he had
better be left to sleep."

I stood up and waited for a moment, but it seemed he
had spent his small strength and was already dozing off.
Impulsively, I bent down and pressed my lips to the
back of his hand, then hurried out of the room without
speaking.

I went straight to Roma's room. And when I heard
footsteps following me down the hall, I turned and
locked the door from the inside. The footsteps stopped
and retreated, and I thanked God aloud that André had
enough sensitivity to leave me alone.

There was no doubt that my brief visit with Benjamin
Starr had had a profound effect upon me. For one
thing, the old man himself, valiantly struggling to regain
some of his lost power, had touched me deeply. I would
do what I could to give him a reason for living—as
Roma would have done. And perhaps when, and if, the
time came for him to know the truth, he could transfer a
bit of his love to me, the real me. Subconsciously, I
think, I longed for this. For doesn't everyone, even
someone without a memory, long for the love of a
father?

But there was another thing. For the very first time since I had awakened in the hospital, something had touched my memory. I couldn't say exactly what— whether it was the sight of the old man lying in the bed, or the dark furniture, or perhaps even the way the light fell across the floor. I don't know. But something, something vague and wonderful and frightening, something ineffable, had passed through me.

I still remembered nothing, but it seemed like a beginning. And after all the failures of the doctors, it was like a miracle. I was exultant. I felt as though I had taken the first step of a momentous journey. And somehow now I had to continue. Perhaps the way forward led backward, too.

And so in triumph and in hope, I prepared for a stay in the great house high on a hill overlooking an ocean that I had only seen in my dreams.

I moved with a new firm step toward the French windows and the little balcony that André had twice fled to. This time I opened them wide and stepped out myself. I took a long deep breath of the bracing air and stood still.

For the first time within my brief memory, I contemplated the future with less fear than hope. It gave me a strength I had never known. I stood there until the chill of dusk forced me to turn back into the room.

An overpowering sleepiness came to me almost immediately. I quickly got out of my clothes and slipped between the covers of the bed, exhausted.

One day—one day had passed.

CHAPTER SEVEN

I AWOKE RESTED and refreshed and with excitement running through me. It was as though I was about to start a new life. It had not turned out as I had planned, for I had never meant to impersonate Roma, but the die was cast. And perhaps if I spent a week or two helping Benjamin, sparing him the shock of Roma's death, I would feel that I had done one last thing for Roma. Then I could look forward to the future, my own future.

But I ate the breakfast Emma brought me with a nervous eye on the dressing room. I would have to speak to André about that wildcat. I didn't see why they couldn't keep him downstairs if they had to keep him. Every minute in the room left me uncertain. When I stepped out of bed and wanted to dress, would Satan pounce on me? How could I escape his evil eye, or perhaps his claws?

Cautiously, after finishing my breakfast, I rose and looked around the room. Satan was not in his bed. I went into the dressing room and opened the closet doors, standing well back in case he should fly out. No cat—at least he couldn't be seen. But I couldn't be sure. Did I dare put my hand in and pull out a garment?

I sighed with relief when Emma came back for my tray. But I realized just in time that if I was to play the part that André wanted me to, the part of Roma, I couldn't reveal how I felt about Satan. I spoke as she lifted the tray.

"Have you seen Satan this morning, Emma?"

She stopped and looked at me. "As a matter of fact, I have, ma'am. And now that you're home, maybe you can do something about it."

"About what?" I asked shakily.

"Well, I don't think it right. He comes in whenever he gets the chance, slips right in. I never know how he does it, but he likes to get up on Mr. Benjamin's bed and sleep. He's there now. He makes me nervous. I don't dare touch him. But maybe you—"

"Oh," I interrupted her, "just leave him there. I'm sure Grandfather likes the company. I don't think he'll do any harm."

"Well all right, ma'am, if you say so. But I don't think the doctor would approve."

"We'll see, Emma. Don't worry."

With a sense of relief, I returned to the dressing room. As she left, I dashed to the bath, showered quickly and then ran to the closet. Not hesitating this time, I chose a powder-blue sweater and skirt, along with some flat-heeled shoes, and dressed quickly.

I had already finished brushing my hair, letting it fall gently in its own way off my face, when I remembered that I had to keep it forward, over my ears. Quickly I made the change, not really liking it. Perhaps I would get used to it.

Then I stood up. I was ready. But ready for what? I went to the windows and opened them, instinctively reaching for the ocean. Would I dare go out there?

Before I had time to answer my own question, I saw a figure waving at me from the rocks on the beach. It was André. Immediately he began to run toward the house, then disappeared. I barely had time to come in from the balcony, when the door flew open and he was in the room with me.

He rushed toward me, bringing with him the smell of the ocean, and stopped short a few feet away. I still like to rememoer him as he was that morning, for it was a rare moment. I scarcely recognized him. That dark and tragic look that had seemed to be stamped on his face was washed away. I saw before me a tousled youth, years younger than he had looked the previous day, dressed in a scarlet turtleneck sweater and blue jeans covered with smudges of paint. His black hair still seemed to be flying in the wind, and his skin for the first time showed glints of color. But most of all, his eyes were changed. Those steely blue eyes were actually shining.

"Come," he said. "I've been waiting for you." And he stretched out his hands toward me in a gesture of friendship.

I stepped toward him, responding, when he suddenly looked down at his hands and pulled them back.

"Sorry," he apologized, "they're a mess. I've been painting again. First time in a long while."

Then, as he wiped his hands with a handkerchief, he added, "You've inspired me."

I was embarrassed for some reason. I turned away and started to talk about Satan.

"That cat," I said, "I'm scared of him. Can't you keep him somewhere else?"

"I'm afraid not. He's Roma's baby. She wouldn't have had him anywhere but here."

"But he's on Benjamin's bed now."

"I know. When Roma and I went away, they say he seemed drawn to Benjamin, but his home is here, in this room."

"Emma doesn't like it. She's afraid of him. So am I."

"Everybody is. Just leave him alone, and don't let

him know you're afraid. Now come; I want to show you around. You ought to know the house.''

He pocketed his handkerchief and grasped my hand, leading me out of the room.

What is there about the touch of the hand that can convey so intimately the mystery, the intricacies of one who, a moment before, was a stranger? It was as though, through some telepathy of the fingers, I *knew* André and, at the touch of his hand, trusted him. And so, with a new feeling of euphoria, I allowed him to lead me down that beautiful curving staircase to the lower floor.

"I want you to see the house," he was saying. "It's a grand old place. Roma did a great deal of redecorating, but most of the old things are still here. You'll see the antiques and the heirlooms mixed in with the modern things.''

We were standing in the foyer, the front entrance, and I admired the dark hardwood floors, mahogany table and large crystal chandelier over the doorway.

We walked to the right and entered the enormous living room. It was elegant yet comfortable, with an ancient flagstone fireplace, two great pale green couches, oyster-white carpet, white draperies, a marble-top coffee table and a grandfather clock.

On seeing this room, I realized in a rush how hungry I was for a home. What a terrible emptiness lay in me. But it was the clock—the great antique grandfather clock—that drew me. Leaving André, I crossed the room, and stood before it. Just as I did, it struck the hour in a small, bell-like tone, and a queer feeling ran through me, that same indescribable sensation I had had in Benjamin's room. Was it possible that I had seen a clock like this before? But where? Certainly not at the hospital. I wanted to stand there and feel what was inside me as I looked at it, but André came up to me and started to talk about it.

"Such a beautiful thing," he was saying, "really rare. Been in the family for generations. But don't try to tell time by it—at least not in the summer."

"Isn't it working right? It looks in fine condition."

"Oh, the best. But Grandfather Benjamin doesn't believe in daylight saving—he keeps it on "God's time" all year round, no matter what the rest of the world does. It gets a little confusing...."

He laughed and took my hand and led me to the dining room.

This room was elegant too—fruitwood French Provincial table and chairs, the same oyster-white carpeting and once more a sparkling crystal chandelier overhead. An impressionistic painting, a mass of mysterious colors that looked like Paris in the sun, hung over the buffet.

I barely glanced at the next, a games room. It contained a billiard table, several chairs, and a card table in the corner, all rather forlorn looking. Who would play games in this house now?

Next to the games room was a library. Ah! This room invited me. It was an "old" room again, untouched by change. I wanted to stay. How easily I could see myself sprawled out on one of the huge brown leather sofas in front of the flagstone fireplace, or staring out the picture window on the side facing the ocean, a book in my lap.

And then there were the paintings. Wherever books did not line the walls, there were paintings—oils and watercolors. I felt my pulse quickening as I looked. Could these be André's paintings? They felt like him—moody, bursting with feeling. At some spots the brush seemed to have slashed at the canvas uncontrollably; at others it became meticulously gentle and precise. The artist had caught the movement, the violence and the mystery of the sea. But there were no people in his pictures, which bothered me.

"Are they yours?" I questioned.

He acknowledged them with a shrug.

"They're beautiful, but...."

"But?" he quizzed.

"I expected—I don't know why—I thought you would do portraits."

"What made you think that?"

His tone was sharp, and I thought I had offended him. "I don't know. Forgive me. I really like these."

He looked at me closely then. "You're right, you know. I used to do portraits. Only portraits. But I gave it up."

I didn't answer, and after staring at me for a minute, he looked away and said in a strained voice, "I found myself doing the same face all the time. So I gave it up."

We were silent for a time; then he turned back to me abruptly. "Well, if it's portraits you want, look at this one."

He led me to the center of the far end of the room. "Here," he said, as he pointed to a dark painting with a heavy gilt frame. "Here is a portrait."

Indeed it was. Smooth, dark and traditional. A picture of a young man. I stood staring at it. When I didn't say anything, he asked, "Don't you recognize him?"

"Why should I recognize him?" But strangely, after staring a minute more, I did.

"It's Benjamin," I said, "when he was a young man!"

"Not quite right. He's Benjamin's son." Then, after a significant pause, he added, "He's...your father."

He couldn't have known what a wave of emotion he sent through me! *Your father!* How the words pierced me! But almost immediately I realized he had meant Roma's father. He was making sure I remembered who I was supposed to be.

I tried to slough off the deep depression that suddenly overcame me. I continued to stare at the picture as though memorizing it.

And then I noticed, right next to it, the fading marks of another frame, which had been taken down. I was about to remark about it, when there was a knock on the door. It was the maid.

"Excuse me, sir, but there's a phone call for you."

André turned from me and moved toward a phone in the corner. "I'll take it here."

Susan disappeared, and I waited while he picked up the phone.

"Who?" he exploded. Then, "You're *where*? Well…of course, I'll come. I'll pick you up. No, no, don't; I'll come. Just wait there."

He hung up. And there was the old André again, the one I had seen through the glass in the hospital door. The one whose moods I had wrestled with yesterday. The gloomy thunderous André, the man who frightened me.

"Damn," he swore, "damn, damn, damn!"

I stood, tense again, the fleeting relief I had enjoyed this morning all gone.

"So." He paused and looked at me in that penetrating way. "We are not to be alone after all."

I began to tremble again, quaking inside, feeling the precariousness of my position, drowning in uncertainty.

"Clara and James are at the station."

He said it as though doomsday had arrived. "Come," he said, and he took my hand, roughly this time, and hurried me up the stairs and back into Roma's room.

As he closed the door, I caught my breath and was about to demand an explanation. But I didn't have to.

"Listen," he said at once, "it's your stepmother and her son. I mean, Roma's stepmother. Her father married a second time—I told you that. Well, she's coming here. Damn!"

He turned from me and paced the room. I waited.

Finally he stopped and faced me, and I knew he had come to some conclusion.

"Well," he said, his voice hard again, "we're just going to have to ride it through. I'm not going to lose you now—or Benjamin either."

I felt a sudden queasiness as he grasped my arms and sat me down on the edge of the bed. He sat beside me.

"Now listen. Clara, that's Roma's stepmother, is at the station with her son, James. You'll have to call her Aunt Clara. She found out, from God knows where, that Roma had had an accident, and she called the house. Marie told her about Benjamin's stroke, and she offered to come down and help her with him. That was a few days ago, before Marie collapsed. Now she's here with her son. It's too damn bad, but we're going to have to put up with them for a while."

"Will that be so terrible?" I asked the question to release my own tension.

He looked at me critically, as though I were slow-witted. Then he answered with irritation, "It won't be good; I can tell you that. We'll have to be careful. Above all, we can't let them know you're not Roma. Not yet."

"You mean...." Shock was making my throat dry. "You mean you want me to deceive them, too?"

"We can't trust them. We mustn't tell them."

"But why not? I can't pretend—"

"Yes, you can. For Benjamin. For me."

"For *you*!" It came out in a shriek, and I saw him blanch. He couldn't seem to understand that I still regarded him as the enemy, the enemy who had neglected Roma, going off to seek another girl, and perhaps through that neglect, had killed her.

"Just listen and I'll try to explain," he said impatiently. "I don't know these two. I have never met them, but it's because of what Roma told me that I know we could never trust them with what we have to do to save Benjamin."

"What did she tell you?"

He ignored the question and repeated, "It's because of what Roma told me that I know they would rather have him dead than alive."

"What a thing to say!"

"Clara said it. She actually said it to Roma. She hates Benjamin for being alive and old while his son, her husband, was young and is dead."

"I've heard people say things like that. It's only grief."

"Grief. . . and greed. She was angry because she felt fate had dealt her an unfair hand. For if Benjamin had died before his son, which one would have expected, *she* would have inherited half of Benjamin's property. This way, she has only a small annuity, for Roma's father had very little of his own."

"I don't see how all this concerns me."

"Once they know that Roma is out of the way, they will *want* the old man to die."

"But why?"

"To get his money, of course. After his son died, he told Roma that he was leaving everything to her, but if anything happened to her, it would all go to them. Foolishly, for she was very young, Roma told James, and James told his mother. But instead of pleasing her, it enraged her, for she thought she would surely die before Roma. Not only would she have to live modestly in her own lifetime, but James would be left with nothing. But now...." He stopped short and seemed to clench his teeth.

"But now," I finished for him, "they *will* get the money."

He stood up then and seemed to be speaking to himself. "Unless, of course, Benjamin has changed his will. Or gets well enough to change it now."

"Why should he want to change it?"

"Why not?" He turned his head and looked down at me, a curious indignation in his eyes. "A lot of things have changed since Clara and James lived here. Roma grew up and got married."

There was a silence. An awesome silence. And I whispered, half under my breath, "And died."

He whirled on me then in a sudden temper.

"Yes. She died. She's dead. And those scheming devils won't give a damn if Benjamin dies. The sooner the better. They'll be delighted at their good fortune. But I won't have it, I tell you! You've got to help me. You've got to pretend you're Roma until he is out of danger."

His sudden fury frightened me—all the more because an ugly light was dawning on me. He didn't want to keep Benjamin alive because he loved him, but because he wanted to be sure that he'd changed his will!

He didn't want Clara and James to inherit the fortune. He thought he, as Roma's husband, should have it....

And for this he was willing to use me, to involve me, to incriminate me. What would happen to me if Clara and James discovered what I was doing? I had been rash and foolish enough to take Roma's passport. But to add to it this—this *fraud*—so he could inherit a fortune! No!

"I can't do it," I burst out, "I can't."

"But I've explained to you. . . ."

"Yes, you've explained. That's the trouble. I see what you're up to now. And I can't do it."

"What do you mean 'what I'm up to'? I'm simply—"

"You're simply *using* me for your own ends!"

"I'm asking you to help save an old man's life."

"That's what you told me last night—and I believed you. But now I see it is for your own ends, and you don't care what happens to me."

"But I do. That's why. . . ."

He moved toward me, and I sprang away from him across the room, in my agitation. My tension and anger were mounting, overriding my fear.

"Suppose those two people should discover me as a fraud, an imposter. They would be furious. They would nave me arrested, prosecuted. They could accuse me of wanting to *really* pass myself off as Roma."

"I would never let that happen."

"How do I know? How can I trust you? I would be in an impossible position."

"You're in an impossible position now."

"Ves, I am. And I'm leaving. I won't stay here and be your patsy."

And I turned and walked into the dressing room. determined to find my own clothes and leave even if I had to fight my way out.

He came thundering up in back of me.

"I see I can't reason with you. You've got some nonsense in your head. But I won't let you ruin every-thing now. You will stay and you will do as you're told."

"You can't make me," I retorted.

"I can call the police right now. I can tell them what you've already done."

We glared at each other, I from inside the narrow

dressing room, he standing in the arched doorway, blocking it.

And then, after a long tense minute, with an almost incredible change of attitude, he added, "Please.. please don't spoil everything."

The gentle pleading in his voice unhinged me. I sank down in the little chair and dropped my head into my hands, suddenly physically ill.

I felt him come up behind my chair. "You've got to go through with it, Roma." He used the name as though he really believed it was mine. "You've got to. There are good reasons. Trust me."

I sat there, limp, while he went on talking. He was saying something about Clara and James not having seen Roma since she was sixteen. Five years ago, years in which she had grown up. They wouldn't be surprised if I seemed different. There would be no danger of their guessing. They would accept me, as Benjamin had.

I heard him only in a very vague way, as an undertone to my thoughts. I couldn't figure him out. I *wanted* to believe him, but how could I? He had revealed, hadn't he, that *he* was a scheming devil—scheming for a fortune and willing to use me to secure it.

And then, in the midst of these thoughts, another, even more horrifying one, came to me. Suppose Benjamin should die suddenly—tonight—leaving his fortune to Roma because he thought she was still alive. Would André let me confess that I was not Roma then? Or would he want me to continue this charade so that "we" would inherit the money instead of Clara and James?

My head was reeling. I felt a web closing around me, and knew I had to get out before it grew too strong to break. But I was afraid of André now. I knew in my heart I was no match for him. So I let him finish giving me instructions.

"Just do as I say, and we'll come out all right. Remember, they haven't seen Roma for five years, though they have kept in touch. It will be better if you stay up here, in bed, or at least in the room. They know you've had an accident. I'll try to keep them away, but if you have to see them, don't worry. They'll never know the difference. Just believe me, it's the best way...if we want to save Benjamin."

At those last words, I stood up and walked past him back into the bedroom. There were tears in my eyes that I did not want him to see. For a little while I had believed in him as a good man, a man with human feelings, who wanted to save an old man great pain and shock. But now disappointment and shame and, yes, fear, were raging inside me. There was nothing I could say to him.

I stood stiffly while he came up to me and spoke in that voice so soft and resonant, the voice that had fooled me into believing in him.

"Be good. Please. Stay here and help me. Everything will turn out all right. Believe me. I've got to go now. They're already at the station."

Then he crossed the room and left.

CHAPTER EIGHT

I WAITED, TENSE, till I heard the front door close and a car start up. Then I sprang into action. There was only one thing to do: leave this house. I had to run, hide. Never come near here agian.

I pulled off Roma's blue sweater and skirt and began to look around for my own things. As I looked I castigated myself. Incredible that I should have got myself into a situation such as this. Intolerable! I should have left immediately, because how could it all end? I could see nothing but disaster for me.

I tore through the clothes closet, hunting for my poor little black dress, so drab alongside Roma's display. And there it was, hanging forlornly at the very rear, next to my tweed coat.

I tore it off the hanger and slipped into it, found my own black shoes and took my coat.

Now, if I could find my purse and my flight bag, I would be ready to go. I looked around and at first saw neither of them, berating myself as I opened drawers here and there. What was the matter with me? Why hadn't I thought of them yesterday when I first woke up? Why hadn't I demanded to know where my things were? I should have been able to put my hands on them immediately. I was wasting time. I didn't know how long André would be. I didn't know how far the station was from here. I didn't know. . . .

And then I found my purse. It was in the top drawer

of the dresser. Relieved, I pulled it out and continued the search for my flight bag.

I looked everywhere, in every drawer and in every closet corner. No bag. As I looked, panic began to sweep through me. My flight bag, my little innocent-looking canvas flight bag, held the most precious possession I had. It held my ring. My satyr ring, locked in the little black Japanese box. But where was it? Where *was* it?

I grew frantic as I continued searching, opening every drawer (even the ones I knew were too small to hold the bag), poking in every corner of the closet, sweeping things aside recklessly, reaching up to top shelves, crawling on my knees among the shoes.

When I didn't find it, I began to shake, to break out in a cold sweat. Still I looked. Over and over around the room again and again until I was dizzy.

Finally I had to face it. There was no bag anywhere in the room. I stood there, my hand taut over my mouth because I thought I might scream.

Suddenly finding my ring took precedence over everything else. I had to find it before I could leave the house, because nothing would matter if that were lost. Nothing. My ring was a lifeline, my only tie to a past I hoped some day to regain. I had to have it, to hold onto it in order to live.

How foolish to have left it in a box! Never mind what the doctors had said about putting it out of sight. Never mind the pain of trying to remember. I should have put it on my finger and loved it, loved my pain, because it was all I had. It was my life.

There was only one hope for me now if I were to leave before André came back. Perhaps Emma, or Susan, had put it somewhere. I would find out.

I had already crossed the room and had my hand on

the doorknob when I stopped. I couldn't go to Benjamin's room dressed to leave. Emma would wonder. Perhaps she would even try to stop me. I couldn't explain everything to her.

Quickly I pulled off my dress and slipped into the first long robe I put my hand on, a suitable dark brown wraparound. I even remembered to kick off my shoes and step into bedroom slippers. Then, with an effort to quiet my wildly beating heart, I left the room and went down the hall to Benjamin's room. I knocked lightly and then opened the door.

Emma was standing with a tray in her hand, and at the sight of me, I think she almost dropped it.

"Mrs. Tate," she said, "what's the matter?"

I realized then that I must have looked rather frantic, but there was nothing I could do about it.

"Have you seen my little flight bag?" I asked abruptly. "It's a little canvas case. I had it when I came home, but now I can't find it."

She continued to look at me strangely and put the tray down. "I didn't see any flight bag when Mr. Tate brought you in. He carried you up the stairs. Susan took your purse, I remember, and your hat—but I didn't see anything like a flight bag."

She didn't know that she was sounding a kind of death knell for me. My knees began to buckle.

"You had better sit down, ma'am." She led me to a chair. "You look ill."

I couldn't answer her, and she continued, "I'm sure Mr. Tate will know where it is. And I'll ask Susan. I was just about to go down with this tray."

She stood by my side for a moment, and I made a great effort to appear normal. "Would you?" I said. "Would you ask Susan? It's important to me. I'll stay here with Grandfather Benjamin. Please go."

She left, a little reluctantly, looking back at me and telling me she thought Benjamin was asleep.

But he wasn't. As soon as she closed the door, he opened his eyes and turned his head toward me.

It was like an invitation, and without thinking, I ran over to him and knelt by his bed. Like a little girl I dropped my head against his enormous frame, and suddenly I was weeping. I knew it was the last thing I should do, to upset a sick man that way. But in that second the trauma I had been through with André, the whole experience of being in this house, overwhelmed me. It was as though having this old man close to me broke the cords of my restraint.

I struggled unsuccessfully to quiet myself, to suppress my sobs, until I felt a movement, a touch on my head. I looked up and stopped instantly.

"Grandfather!" The word sprang naturally from my lips. "You've moved your hand!"

His lips turned upward a bit in a little crooked smile. Then he struggled to form the words: "What...is... the...matter?"

Shame flashed through me. I should not have let him see me this way. I should be a comfort and strength to him.

"I'm all right now," I said quickly, brushing my tears away. "I'm fine. I was just so...so glad to see you!" Strange as it sounded, that was completely true.

"And now," I added brightly, "you've moved your hand!"

He wiggled the fingers of his right hand and then moved his head toward the left. "But...not...this one."

His left side lay still as death. We both stared for a second at it, and then I began to massage him.

"I'll help it. I'll make you better."

It was an impulse, and I acted on it at once. I knelt there by his bedside, pressing my fingers into his flesh. I started slowly, gently on his fingers. How large and how strong they were despite their limpness. If I could only bring them back to life!

I massaged his hand and his arm all the way up into his shoulder, very, very gently.

He was aware of what I was doing, and he smiled in appreciation, watching me through half-opened eyes.

And as I worked, something was happening to me. I was growing peaceful and quiet inside. A great many thoughts were forming in me. I seemed able to think more clearly than I had before.

About my ring. Of course I had to find it. No matter how long it took, I would track it down. But if Emma should come up with it in a few moments, should I— could I—leave Benjamin now?

I looked down at his kind face, hollow with age, and felt an indescribable pull. There was something about this old man that had more power over me than even André did. It was as though he really were my grandfather. Even more, as though we had ties that could not be explained. Was it mutual need?

At any rate, I was back where I had been this morning. The die was cast. I would stay. Even if André's motives were not the purest, what did it matter if I helped to save Benjamin?

Only, I vowed silently, only great personal danger would make me run away. But for now, I would try to be Roma Starr for Benjamin, for André, and even for Clara and James.

With the decision a kind of peace came over me. My hands still at last, I sat there quietly, only half-aware, when suddenly, without a knock, the door was flung open, and I faced a tall, handsome, blond young man.

I remained where I was, by Benjamin's side, staring. He stared, too, for a second, before he broke the spell. Then he cried, "Roma! It's you! You're here!"

And he rushed to me. I was glued to the spot, but he lifted me up and hugged me until I thought my ribs would break, kissing me all over my face and neck.

"Roma," he repeated over and over, "Roma! My God, it's good to see you!"

He looked at me then, holding me at arm's length.

"You poor kid! I can see you've been through a lot. But André told us you'd be in bed. And here you are, up and about!"

I couldn't seem to get a word out. I was struck dumb. He went on. "Good Lord, Roma, don't you know me? Say 'Hello James'; say *something*!"

But I couldn't. It was André's angry voice that rescued me. "What in God's name are you doing in here?"

And then I put my hand to my head. The room was going around. I had had too much this morning. I didn't know whether I would have fainted or not, but André took the opportunity to pick me up and carry me back to Roma's room. On the way I heard him telling James that I had to be left alone. And then the door closed and he placed me on the bed.

"Well," he said as I opened my eyes, "it's a damn good thing you fainted—or pretended to."

"I didn't pretend!"

"I tried to protect you. I told them you were still convalescing. And I told you to stay in this room and let me handle it."

His high-handed tone angered me. The blood came rushing back to my head, leaving me no longer faint.

"I had to see Benjamin. He needed me. Isn't that the reason I'm here? To help him? Isn't that what you told me?"

I could see he caught the challenge in my tone, and for a moment a dark look of pain flickered in his face. Then he admitted at last, "Yes, of course. That's the reason you're here." He added brusquely, "There's no harm done. I guess you'll have to see them. Just don't let them bully you. You'll have to remember that *you* are the mistress here. I'll help. I'll tell you all I can. But don't do anything foolish. And don't trust them."

Strange, that he should say that at the very time I was distrusting him most. I was just about to question him about my flight bag when he turned away and looked about the room.

It was certainly in a shambles. In my frantic search, I had left drawers half-open, their contents spilled out, and even my own coat and dress thrown over the chair.

I could see the questioning look in his eyes, coupled with a kind of dismay when he looked back at me.

"What have you been doing? What have you been searching for?"

I rose on one elbow, and my voice shook as I said, "I've been looking for my flight bag. I had it in my hand when I fainted at the airport."

"Good Lord!" He threw up his hands. "Did you tear the room up just for that?"

His concern about the room incensed me. I sat up, tense. "Where is it? Do you have it?"

"What's so important about that case?" He was brushing me aside. "You have everything you need here."

And he started to tidy things up, closing the drawers, putting things away. I rose from the bed and followed him about.

"André, answer me. Where is my flight bag? I've got to have it."

"Don't be so frantic. We'll probably find it."

"Probably! You mean you've lost it!"

"I didn't say that. I'm sure it's not lost."

"Then where is it? I had it when I left the plane. You must have seen it."

He had finished with the drawers, and he went over to the chair and picked up my dress and coat. He looked at them suspiciously, and I knew that he knew why I had had them out.

"What were you doing with these?" he asked.

"They're mine," I answered defiantly, "I thought I might wear them."

"Not here! As long as you're here, you're Roma and you wear her clothes."

I snatched my coat and my dress from his hands.

"Yes, as long as I'm here," I said significantly. Then I went into the dressing room and hung them up myself.

He followed me and stood behind me while I put them on hangers. As I turned around, I got back to the question of my flight bag.

"You haven't answered me: where is my flight bag?"

He was very close to me, towering over me, and he placed his hands in a tight grip on my arms.

"Please," he said, and there was genuine pleading in his voice, "please don't try to run away now. It would be a great mistake."

"Mistake for whom?" I asked skeptically.

And he answered, "For both of us. For all of us.'

We stood there in the narrow confines of the dressing room; I, glowering upward into his face, he, looking down into my eyes.

After a minute his grip loosened, and I felt his arms around me, pressing me to him softly, tenderly And slowly the iron in me melted, and I leaned against him willingly.

He kissed my head, then I heard his faint cry: "Oh, God, God!"

Something in it pierced me. It was a cry of longing, and even in my own distress, I was moved to wonder about the great pain that this strange elusive man harbored.

I, who was so full of pain and longing myself, felt a kind of compassion, a kind of empathy with him. But there was nothing I could say. There was no way I could express the thing between us, even to myself.

We stood clasped together for a few moments, and then he seemed to come back to reality. He pushed me from him gently.

"We'll find your case. You're not to worry."

But I was worried. "But where is it, if it isn't here? Did you leave it at the airport?"

"We'll see. I have to go down to Boston tomorrow on business. I'll stop at the airport, I promise. But tell me—you must tell me—" he took my hands in his and looked straight into my eyes with a deep, inquiring stare "—what is so important to you in that case?"

Confronted with the direct question, I faltered. I couldn't reveal to him that all my life's hope, my past and my future, was tied up in a box in that little flight bag.

I couldn't say, "There is a ring in that case that holds a secret. One day, through that ring, I'm going to find out who I am. I'm not Sara Smith any more than I'm Roma Starr." So I was silent. I lowered my eyes and pulled my hands from between his.

"It's just that—it's my property. I need it."

I heard him sigh as I walked away from him.

Just before he left, he said, "Don't worry about your case. I'm very good at finding—" He stopped there and said in a husky half-whisper, "Lost objects. Trust me." That seemed to be one of his favorite phrases. But could I trust him?

CHAPTER NINE

THAT NIGHT I DREAMED my old dream again. It began, as usual, with the face of my ring leering up at me, then the fingers of the setting unwinding and beckoning to me. I followed the silent gesture until I was wandering amid all those empty rooms again, all open to the sky. As I wandered, arms outstretched, I began to call. "Where are you? Where are you?" and then the scene changed, and I was facing that wild and craggy seacoast—my seacoast.

Only this time, mixed in with all this, were faces, a kaleidoscope of faces, clicking by one after the other till finally I recognized one. It was Grandfather Benjamin, old Benjamin Starr. I tried to hold onto him, to bend over him and hug him, but his face disappeared like the rest, only to be followed by André's.

As it came closer and closer, and became larger and larger, his expression changed from the gloomy, diabolical one that had first impressed and frightened me, to a smiling and then laughing, almost mocking, look.

Terrified, I pulled back from it, and as it seemed to bear down on me, I tried to run, but my legs were like lead; I couldn't move. Then, as his face pressed closer, almost touching mine, it evaporated and emerged again as the face on my ring. It grew larger and larger until. like a balloon, it exploded before my widening eyes.

I woke up screaming, screaming so loud that I must have awakened the household. In a few minutes the room seemed to be full of people. Someone lit a lamp.

The first to arrive was James, in robe and pajamas. Before I could recover from my dazed awakening, he was by my bedside, leaning over me, asking, "What's the matter? What's the matter?"

Then came Emma, robe flying as she ran toward me, authoritatively pushing James aside and putting her arms around me. My screams had changed to sobs by that time, and I remember that I nestled into her as a child does into a mother, burying my head in her breast.

Then I heard someone running and André's breathless voice asking, "What's going on here? What's the matter, Roma?"

I stopped sobbing then. I was back. Back to the reality of this very unreal situation I was in. I would have to get hold of myself.

"It's nothing," I said at last, like a child excusing herself. "It was just a bad dream. A nightmare."

I could hear a collective sigh throughout the room. And then I heard an unfamiliar voice—a woman's voice I hadn't heard before. It cut cleanly into the night on a high-pitched note.

"Why is she being left alone at night? If she's just out of the hospital, someone should be with her."

Emma spoke up. "I have to be with Mr. Starr."

"Of course. But what about her husband? What about *you*?" The speaker turned to face André squarely, accusingly.

I knew at once that it was Clara. "Aunt" Clara. I looked at her, a formidable figure: tall, almost as tall as André himself, thin as a reed, straight and proud.

Her face struck me rather like the prow of a ship, her chin held high as though facing a perpetual wind; her short black hair brushed back over a high forehead;

her white, white face narrow and sharp of feature, the dark points of eyes peering out of deep sockets.

I could see that she was a woman to be reckoned with. She asked questions, and she demanded answers. But she was not to get a satisfactory one from André that night.

"She's better off alone," he snapped. "She needs complete rest."

Then he turned to me, and there was a warning look in his eye. "You're all right now, aren't you?"

I knew what my answer had to be. "Of course. It was just a silly dream. Forgive me, everyone. Please, go back to bed."

"There. Now everyone, go. She'll be all right. I'll see to that."

Emma rose obediently, patting my shoulder affectionately. But James and Aunt Clara were reluctant to leave. I caught James glaring jealously at André. And Clara moved, not away, but toward me, ignoring André.

"Are you sure you're all right, Roma?"

She leaned over me, scrutinizing me. "It's a shame to see you like this after all these years."

And then, with a shake of her head, she added, "You certainly do look peaked. Don't you want me to stay with you?"

"No, thank you, Aunt Clara," I answered, forcing myself to use this intimacy. "I'm really quite all right. Please, go back to bed."

At that she suddenly pulled her lips together like a drawstring bag and kissed me. Then she straightened up and sailed out of the room.

I lay still until I heard James trail out after her and the door close. André crossed back over to me and asked in a low voice, "Are you really all right? Do you want me to stay?"

I groaned. Why should I want him to stay? It was his face that had given me the nightmare. And yet, I couldn't say, "Go." Perhaps I did want him to stay. After all, strange as it seemed, he was my only "friend" in a friendless world.

I did not protest when he sat on the edge of the bed. After a minute he leaned over and put his hand over mine. Then he said softly, "My dear, you must forgive me. One day you *will* forgive me. I know it has been a terrible strain on you."

I couldn't believe my ears. Was this the unfeeling André from whom I had fled, before whom I had fainted, beneath whose frightening gaze I had reconciled myself to my current situation?

I remained silent, lying there and looking out into the dimly lit room, listening to the ticking of the little gold clock on the night table and the distant splashing of the ocean against the rocks. Time seemed to drift away, and I neither moved nor spoke. Everything took on an unreal quality, even more unreal than my amazing two-day stay in this house.

I began to feel André's presence invading me, and I finally turned my head to look at him. He was staring at me, but with a far-off look in his eyes. He was looking at me, but he was somewhere else, somewhere I couldn't reach him.

All at once I was reminded of Roma's response when I had asked her if she was traveling with anyone: *"I thought so. But he was always too far away. He'll always be—too far away."*

Looking at him now, I knew a little of what she must have felt. To love this man would be to suffer. Innocent and unfamiliar with love as I was, I knew by instinct that no woman could stand for long being so cut off from the focus of the man she loved.

Suddenly I made a move toward him. I had to try to penetrate the mystery of this man, to whom I seemed destined, for at least a little while, to be so closely tied.

"André," I began. And then, before I knew it, I felt his lips pressed deep into the palm of my hand. They were warm and soft and oh, so tender. I was completely paralyzed until he raised his lips for a moment. Then I tried to make some movement, some response. But before I could voice a sound, he had pulled me to him and closed his strong arms around me in a fierce embrace.

In that moment I felt a cosmic love for him—the kind of all-encompassing love that one feels for another. I did not resist. It was like a balm to my lonely soul. If I could have believed he was loving *me*, I would have given myself to him forever. But I was awakened from my beautiful dream by his mumbling, "Oh, God—oh, Sybil, Sybil!"

I stiffened and pushed him from me. I tried to hide the anger that rose in me. I had pitied Roma for loving him. Now was I to pity myself? Who was this Sybil anyway? Suddenly I had to know.

"Who is she?" I asked abruptly. "Who is this Sybil you can't forget?"

I half expected him to flare at me or to jump up and leave. But after a moment of taut silence, he answered. "Someone I have loved—and lost."

"Lost? How?"

"The gods destroyed us."

"Don't talk in riddles. Tell me what happened."

"If I thought it would do any good, believe me, I would tell you—everything."

His voice went through me. It was a single hollow note of despair. I softened.

"It's always good to talk things out. I learned that at the hospital. You must tell someone. Tell me."

He turned toward me then and nestled his head against my shoulder. I could feel his hair brushing my cheek. Part of me wanted to run my fingers through it. But part of me held back.

"Tell me," I repeated. "Talk to me."

It was as though I had struck a nerve. He twisted his head and glared accusingly at me. "Talk to *you*! If I only could!"

This time I stiffened, hurt. "Why *can't* you talk to me?"

"Because. . . you wouldn't understand."

He said it between grinding teeth. His bitterness, incredibly, seemed directed toward me. But grief, I have learned since then, does different things to different people. Some weep, some despair. Others, like André, carry anger around with them like a shield. I had cracked his armor and he let his anger tumble out at me.

"I trusted her," he raged, "and she betrayed me. She promised she would never forget me—" Suddenly he stopped, then added flatly, "But there's no use talking to you."

I tried to overcome this personal rebuff. "You mean she fell in love with somebody else?"

He gave me a scathing look. "I told you you wouldn't understand."

Then he turned and buried his head in my shoulder again. This time I did put out my hand and run it through his hair. I didn't know what else to do. I concluded his Sybil must have died.

After a while I asked quietly, "Didn't it help when you married Roma? Didn't you love her—a little?"

"Oh, my God," he groaned and got up and left me. He walked to the windows, his back to me.

Perhaps he was right. I couldn't understand him. But after a while he came back to me and sat on the edge of the bed.

"I want to tell you something. I did love Roma—a little. But I married her because I thought she could lay the ghost to rest."

"Lay the ghost to rest?"

"Of Sybil. I told her about Sybil. She thought, we both thought at the time, that she might be the one to make me forget."

After a long pause I ventured, "But she couldn't?"

"No."

Then, so softly that I could barely hear him, he said, "There are some men who love only once—and forever."

There was a terrible silence as the reason for André's hopeless grief sank into my consciousness. To be in love forever—with a ghost!

I didn't know what to say to him after that. He was too far away. He had decided for himself that he was doomed.

But I was no longer angry with him. I had no right to be angry. We were two suffering people, André and I. He, grieving for a lost love; I, grieving for a lost life. Could we ever meet, or did our separate griefs create too wide a breach?

Helplessly, I leaned toward him. "I wish I could help you," I whispered and closed my eyes to hide my own pain.

I could feel him staring at me, could feel him breathing close to my cheek as he leaned toward me. And then his lips pressed against mine and for a moment, just a moment, I allowed myself to return his kiss and melt into his arms.

But at last I pulled away, not wanting to be betrayed, like Roma, into loving a man who could not love me.

At my movement he sat upright and let go of me. "I guess you're all right now," he said in his normal, impersonal voice.

"Yes," I answered shortly, copying his tone.

He stood up, and I knew that he was about to leave.

"I've got to go down to Boston in the morning, on business. I'll be back by evening, or as soon as I can. Try to stay right here in this room while I'm gone. It will be safer. I've told them you're recuperating. They'll understand."

So he was going off and leaving me alone here!

"André," I said, suddenly plunged back to the reality of my own problems. "That woman—Clara—"

"*Aunt* Clara," he interrupted me. "You must remember."

"Very well, Aunt Clara. She frightens me. She'll see right through me."

"She didn't see through you. She accepted you."

"For those few minutes. But the way she stared at me, *through* me...."

"Don't let her bother you. *You* are the mistress here."

"But she knows more about everything than I do. She's more the mistress here than I am."

"You must *believe* in yourself, and she will."

"How can I when I don't know anything? I won't know any of the answers to the questions she might ask me."

"I told you how to handle it. Stay here. In bed, if need be. I've told her you need quiet and rest. You can always pretend to—"

"I'm sick of pretending. I would rather tell her the truth."

He gave an impatient little shrug.

"Tell her the truth, and she'll have you arrested as a fraud and an imposter. You've already compromised yourself, you know."

Yes, I thought bitterly, *I know. I know.*

"And she'll manage to kill Benjamin in the bargain. Are you going to be such a fool?"

A fool, indeed, I thought. *A fool to let you box me in like this.*

As he closed the door after him, another wave of anger rose in me. I was back to hating him.

CHAPTER TEN

I AWOKE THE NEXT MORNING feeling quite ill—feverish and sneezing. And I knew well enough what the doctors back at the hospital would have said: psychosomatic! Of course. I was ill because I couldn't face the day with James and Clara lying in wait for me, so to speak. And André was in Boston. What better excuse to hide behind than a bad cold?

Just the same, I groaned. I really didn't feel well at all.

Emma came in finally, tiptoeing over to my bed. "You've slept late this morning. It's almost noon."

I opened my eyes as she leaned over and touched my forehead. "Why, you're feverish," she said. "Are you ill?"

Just then I sneezed, as if in answer to her question.

"Heavens, the doctor is just leaving. I'll call him back."

"Oh, no—please don't." That was the last thing I wanted. "Just give me a cup of tea and leave me to sleep it off."

"Well, I'll bring you some antihistamine with your breakfast. But if you're not better by tonight, I'll have to call the doctor."

After bringing the tea and the pills, she left me and I dozed off. It was late afternoon when I awoke again.

The sun was soft and fading, throwing prismatic light across those pale sea-foam walls and giving it all a dreamlike quality.

I lay very quietly, listening to the surf, growing accustomed to its music. I glanced lazily about the room, drinking in its soft elegance, and let my gaze fall on the carved fruitwood dresser with the antique candlestick and all the little silver and gold boxes.

And there, in among the boxes, still as they were, lay Satan. Little shivers started down my spine.

He was staring at me as he had that first morning, fixing those wild eyes on me, letting me know that *he* knew I wasn't Roma, and that I had no right to be in her bed.

I had seen him several times, slipping like a shadow in and out of the room when Emma opened the door. He had paid no attention to me. But this time he was concentrating as though he had decided it was time I gave him an account of myself.

I decided the best thing to do was to stare back at him. Neither of us moved an eyelid. I don't know how long our contest would have gone on if it hadn't been interrupted by a knock on the door.

To my relief it opened even before I could answer, and James, looking so handsome in gray flannels and a burgundy sweater, poked his head in.

"May I?" he beamed.

At this Satan jumped noiselessly down and, slowing only to hiss up at James as he passed, slunk out of the room.

"Whew," James breathed, "so that damn wildcat is still here. I hoped he'd be dead by now."

"Hoped?"

He laughed as he approached the bed. "Don't look so surprised; you know how we hated each other. I still bear some nasty scars from that beast. Besides, I'm here to see you, my dear, not the wildcat."

Quickly then he came to me and, leaning over, kissed me open-mouthed.

I was shocked and tried to pull away. At my resistance he let me go but showed no sign of embarrassment. He sat down, still close, on the edge of my bed and looked directly into my eyes.

"It's been damn lonely waiting to see you. Are you feeling any better?"

"Yes, much better," I answered as I pushed him away, "but I'm feverish, I think. Perhaps you had better sit in the chair."

He laughed and rose and pulled one of the chairs up close to the bed. Then he sat and stared at me so steadily that I felt myself growing hot. Finally, with unmistakable intent, he reached out and touched my hand, whispering, "Remember us, Roma?"

I withdrew my hand. "You know I'm married now."

"Yes, I know." Suddenly his face was hard. "Why the hell did you do it? Why didn't you wait for me as you promised? I know you like to play around, but I thought when it came to marrying—"

"People...change," I ventured weakly.

"Change! Yes." The word enflamed him. "Certainly *you* have changed! You don't even *sound* the same with that phony English accent you picked up over there."

"It's not phony." I was stung into defending myself.

"Oh, come on! Of course it is. Why don't you drop it and be yourself." He glowered at me through narrowed eyes.

"You're certainly not the same girl I said good-bye to. Your whole personality has changed. I don't know you anymore. What has that man done to you?"

I felt I was on dangerous ground and struggled for a plausible excuse.

"Well—I've been through a great deal since I last saw you. And then, to top it off, the accident—"

Mention of the accident seemed to soften him.

"God, I'm sorry," he said, "I almost forgot. You look so well and whole. We expected to find you all patched up. The papers said it was a terrible smash."

"The papers?"

"Sure. Didn't you know you were in all the papers? Big splash. You know mother. Reads all the papers—*The Times*, London as well as New York and Boston. She never misses anything, from headlines to obituaries. They gave you quite a write-up: U.S. heiress crashes—Critical condition—Car totaled, and so on."

This was unnerving news for me. I had no idea it had been in the papers.

He went on, "Of course mother called the house right away, but she didn't get any answer. It turned out that Marie and Susan had taken Benjamin to the hospital that night. It took her three days to get Marie. That was when we decided we had better come out and help. We never expected to find you here. Not after that accident. As a matter of fact, I was thinking of going to England to see you as soon as I got mother settled here."

At that I welcomed a gigantic sneeze that shook me and made my eyes water. James handed me a tissue, and I nursed myself as long as I could. As I did, I decided I had better try to change the conversation.

"James, let's not talk about me. Why don't you tell me about you?"

"Me! What is there to talk about, except that I've been waiting for you." And then, irritably, he added, "And why do you keep calling me James? You never called me James before except when you were mad at me."

I panicked. Was it Jim? Jimmy? Jamie? I would have to avoid saying his name at all!

"Oh, please," I begged, turning my head into the pillow and groaning, "I'm tired...."

He reacted angrily. "I see you don't want to talk. But damn it, Roma, you owe me something. You know you do!"

And suddenly he was on my bed again, pulling at my shoulders, turning me around to face him, shaking me.

"I won't have it!" he muttered, "I can't give you up! You're mine! You always were!"

He began to cover me with rough kisses. He wrapped his arms around me, running his hands through my hair as he buried his face in my neck, kissing me, kissing me with a passion that terrified me.

I knew I had to stop him. I tried to push against his body, but I was like a piece of straw in his hands. He had lost control of himself and was holding me down as if about to get his revenge. I had just managed to free one hand and was about to dig my nails into the side of his face, when I heard loud noises coming from down the hall and the sound of someone running.

"Stop it! Stop it!" I cried and managed to pull away just as the knob of my door turned. James flew off my bed as Emma flung open the door. Heaven knows what the two of us would have looked like to her, had she been in any state to notice.

"Hurry!" she cried. "Help!"

I was already out of bed, slipping into my robe, thinking something had happened to Benjamin, when she added, "It's your mother, Mr. James. She's been attacked by that cat."

James immediately grabbed my arm. "You see," he cried, "your damn wildcat is still dangerous. Come on...."

And before I knew it, I was being pulled down the hall toward Benjamin's room. There was nothing l could do but go along, but l felt like an early Christian being thrown to the lions. What could I do about Satan? What good would I be?

Susan had heard the noise and was running up the stairs just as we reached Benjamin's room. We all stood in the doorway. And there was Aunt Clara, cowering against the wall, while Satan, growling fiercely, was standing on a table, his back arched and his bristled fur making him look twice his size. It was plain he had her cornered. James gave me a frantic shove forward.

"Get him down! Get him out of there!"

He seemed to think I would have no problem. But I stood there trembling, with no idea what I could do, or even what Roma would have done.

The cat continued to growl, and Clara shrieked at me, "Take him! Get him away! Hurry! Do something!"

Under this pressure I moved closer, my heart thumping, and did instinctively what anyone would have done had Satan been a tame domestic cat: I clapped my hands loudly and said in as firm a voice as I could command, "Satan!"

At this, startled, he turned his head toward me and let out a vicious snarl. I think he might have sprung at me if it hadn't been for Susan. She jumped between us and cried, "No, no!" causing confusion. And before we knew it, Satan flew off the table and streaked out into the hall.

The crisis was over. There was a palpable sense of relief. Immediately James ran to Clara, and Emma went to Benjamin's side. Susan was saying, "Don't ever take chances when a cat is growling and his fur is ruffled. Not even if it's a *tame* cat. And Satan—he's *wild*."

"Thank you, Susan," I groaned, "you really helped."

James was leaving with Clara on his arm, and I knew I should go with them. Clara was in a state of near hysteria.

"He scratched me! My arm is bleeding. That beast sprang at me, jumped up at me. He could have got my eyes."

"It's all right now, mother. You're safe."

"Safe?" Her voice cracked as it hit a new high. "Safe? I'll never be safe while he's in the house."

She turned toward me then as we went down the hall, and delivered a blistering harangue. "You're a selfish, inconsiderate girl! You always were. You endanger everybody's life with that beast. You saw him ready to jump at me. And what did I do? I tried to protect your grandfather, that's all. He shouldn't be allowed to sleep on the bed with a sick man. You should be ashamed to allow it!"

We had reached her room, and James opened the door. "Come and lie down, mother. Be calm. Roma will get some bandages and iodine and we'll fix you up."

We stepped into what seemed like a garden full of roses. I could almost smell them. It was the wallpaper, large pink roses on a cream background. A great mahogany canopied bed dominated the room. Rose-colored throw rugs lay on the highly polished parquet floor. A chaise lounge upholstered in rose velvet stood by the French windows, which faced the sea.

I waited just inside the door, while James placed his mother on the chaise. I couldn't move; there was something about the room. I was having those queer feelings again: slightly nauseated, slightly giddy. It was a strange, beautiful, but overpowering room, untouched by time.

"Roma!" James's voice was impatient. "Please get the bandages and some iodine. She's bleeding." He was leaning over her, pressing his handkerchief against her arm.

I shook myself awake. Of course I would get the bandages. But where did he expect me to find them? Here? In this room? I hesitated, looking bewildered at four closed doors. Would there be a bathroom with a medicine cabinet behind one of them? Surely. But which one?

"Roma, hurry!"

It jarred me into moving. I opened the first door I came to. It turned out to be a closet, a deep walk-in closet. There were piles of dusty boxes and pictures, and leaning against them was a large old oil painting that seemed to jump out at me. It was a portrait of a beautiful, dark-haired, green-eyed woman wearing a low-necked green dress and a gold medallion around her neck. I stood staring until James called out again. Then I slammed the door shut.

"I'll go get Emma," I said.

"For God's sake!" James jumped up. "We don't need Emma." He came over to me. "What were you doing in the closet?"

He gave me a queer look and then said, "Don't you feel well?"

"I . . . I guess I don't . . . very . . . ."

"You go on back. I'll take care of mother." He hurried to one of the other doors, and as he opened it, I saw a bathroom. He stepped inside and began opening cabinets.

By the time he came out with the bandages and iodine, I had recovered my poise, and I went with him to Clara's side. We both knelt and bathed her arm, pouring on iodine and binding her arm in bandages.

She was stoic, of course. Never a whimper at the iodine, although Satan had given her several deep scratches. By the time we finished, she had fully regained her composure. As I stood up, she stretched herself out regally and leaned her head back against the rose velvet pillows and looked at me.

I was intimidated before she even opened her mouth, but when she raised her eyes and looked at me, peered at me, I knew how an insect must feel under a microscope. Aunt Clara, I was finding out, didn't look; she examined.

"Well," she said at length, "I'm sorry to have disturbed you, Roma."

The way she said it sounded like an accusation. I felt I should apologize for Satan. "I'm sorry, Aunt Clara. I'll try to keep him—"

"My dear, Satan must go. You really can't keep a wild beast in the house any longer. Not with your grandfather ill. Do you know I found him on the bed?"

"But," I ventured, "Grandfather likes to have him there. It's company for him."

"Nonsense. He has plenty of company with all of us here. That animal must go."

She raised her voice, and with an imperious swish of her hand, she repeated, "Do you hear me? I demand that you get rid of him."

At her tone my anger flared like a rocket. I lost all my timidity. "I will do no such thing. Satan is my pet. And this, Aunt Clara, is *my* house."

It came out in a burst as unexpected to me as it was galling to Aunt Clara. She seemed to lose all control. Her body quivered as she rose from the chaise lounge.

"*Your* house! Your house indeed!" Her face grew red and her eyes blazed. "But you have no right to it. You know you have no right to it. It belongs to me. *Me!* My husband should have inherited it—and he would have, if *you* hadn't caused his death...."

"That's ridiculous!" I was defending Roma, of course. "I never caused his death."

"Oh, now you're going to lie about it. Of course, you would! But you didn't then. You knew well enough that your staying out all night, your going out in that sail-boat in that storm, killed him. Your father never would have caught pneumonia if he hadn't spent the night soaking wet, searching for you, trying to rescue you from that...that no-good tramp you went out with!"

I stood open-mouthed, aghast at her released fury. I turned to James. As I did he crossed over to his mother and stood beside her.

"She's right," he said in an angry voice, glaring at me. "You had the decency to feel guilty then. You tried to make it up to mother in your own way. But I see you've changed. You're selfish and unfaithful, and you don't care what happens to us. All you care about is that beach bum you're married to. He doesn't even belong here. *We* belong here. Roma, you know that if your father were alive, when your grandfather dies mother would be mistress here. You can't deny you've robbed her."

Suddenly I realized I was standing there before two enemies. In that moment I understood completely why André could never let them know that Roma was really gone. They were like two scavengers, their claws out-stretched, waiting. Would they wait long to see that Benjamin was finished off? Of course not.

At the same time I felt, in a vague way, that I too was in danger from them. Then I remembered André's tell-ing me that Benjamin planned to leave his fortune to Clara and James if anything should happen to Roma.

I shivered, turned from them and silently left the room.

CHAPTER ELEVEN

AS I CLOSED THE DOOR of Roma's room behind me, I leaned against it and tried to think. My cold, like magic, seemed to have disappeared. My head was clear, but my heart was pounding.

What was I to do now? My rash outburst to Clara had brought everything, every underlying resentment in the two of them, out into the open.

In a way that helped me to have a little more faith in André, in what he had said about them. But it didn't help me to cope with them or with the situation I was in. It was unconscionable of André to leave me alone here, even for a day. He was a heartless creature, that was clear. Where could I go for comfort?

Immediately my thoughts turned to Benjamin, and without a moment's hesitation, I opened the door again and ran down the hall.

I found him alone. He seemed to be sleeping, and Emma must have left for a little rest. I suppose I woke him up, for I went straight to him and put my arms around him and pressed my face to his. I couldn't help it. It was a kind of salve, washing away the meanness of the past few moments.

He groaned and with his half-paralyzed lips tried to kiss me. He eased my heart and I wanted to protect him—from them, from everybody.

"Are you...all right, my dear?"

His speech was improving. It was still thick, but I

could understand him quite clearly. He even tried to smile as I nodded and said, "I'm fine, Grandfather."

Then he said, "The...cat...?"

"Do you mind having him here?" I asked. "Does he frighten you?"

He shook his head. "No. I like him. And...."

"And he likes you." I couldn't help saying it.

"No—only *you*. But he was...lonely, like me, when you went away. Then...he came...to sit with me."

There was a stab in my heart as I leaned over and started to massage his arms. "I shouldn't have gone away," I whispered for the forever silent Roma. "I should never have left you."

As softly as I spoke, he heard me. "Of course...you should. You know I want you...to be...happy."

And then, after a long pause while I worked my fingers into his inert muscles, he whispered, "Is...André making you happy?"

I bit my lip. "Yes, very happy." What else could I say?

"James says...you're not...yourself."

Quickly I was on guard. "I've grown up since James last saw me. Of course I've...changed."

"You've grown...gentler...since you came home. Since you...married André."

He tried to look at me, to see me with his failing eyes. "I wish...I could see you better, my dear. Are you... quite well?"

"Yes, I'm fine. It's you we have to take care of. Don't tire yourself, Grandfather."

"I have to talk. I...have to say...something to you." He paused, gathering strength. I waited, helpless, fearful.

"It's about...your mother. I'm sorry I never talked to you about her. I never let anyone talk to you...."

I could see he was upsetting himself. "It's all right, Grandfather. It doesn't matter."

"Yes, it matters. I'm sorry there was nothing we could do. We tried, your father and I. But now... I wish we had... talked to you. About her.... I never asked you—did you miss her?"

I was trembling by this time. Miss my mother? I didn't even know my mother. We were talking at odds, he about Roma's mother, but the feeling was the same: a feeling of longing and love, of pain and regret—and of something lost.

Then he said, close to my ear, "There's something I want to give you. Something... I should have given you... long ago...."

I grew tense, feeling uneasy. "I don't need anything, Grandfather."

"Yes, you should have them. It's... only right. They... belong. .to you."

I waited while he swallowed and struggled to compose himself. Something in me sensed that this was terribly important to him and difficult for him to do. Something, perhaps, about which he felt guilty.

But my own guilt at being the recipient of anything that should have been Roma's was rising in me. "Please," I begged, "it's not necessary. Don't give me anything."

"You must have them... the letters."

He turned his head toward me but then closed his eyes over tears as he spoke. "Listen carefully... you must go downstairs. The cellar. I hid them... from everybody. I know it was wicked... but I couldn't... it was too late, you see.... I didn't want you to... well, never mind. I want you to have them now. They're from your mother... one to your father, one to you... both unopened. I never opened them. It was... too late... your father had already died...."

I reached out to touch his hand, to ease his agitation while he went on, "They're in the bin—the one marked Number four—there are four bins, you know. They're in a box, in my trunk. Go—get them. Now—while we're alone."

I was petrified. And I had no idea, of course, how to get to the cellar. While I hesitated, wondering what excuse I could give, he continued, "The key to the bin is hidden...it's under a mat...behind the furnace.... Go—please, my dear. I want you to...read them to me."

I was shaking, fearful for him.

"Please," he repeated, "go. I'll wait for you."

I was unspeakably relieved when Emma pushed open the door. She seemed a little surprised to see me.

"Is anything wrong?" she asked. "I didn't mean to be away so long."

"No," I said, rising. "He just wanted to talk a little."

"We mustn't tire him. Now that he's a little better, he tries to do more than he should."

"I'll go," I said.

At that he roused himself. "Roma—do as I ask. I'll be...waiting...for you."

He closed his eyes again as Emma came toward him with some medicine.

As I left the room, my heart was pounding worse than it had been when I entered. How could I do what he asked? I didn't even know how to find the cellar. And then, even if I found the box, it would be wrong for me to read the letters. Surely, I had no right.... And yet, how could I refuse? Why not go right now?

I was in the hall, and no one was about. I started down to the first floor, where I would have to search for the door that would lead to the cellar. Halfway, I panicked, stopped, and held on to the banister. Stairs, all of a sudden, seemed to frighten me. My nerves, no doubt. I brushed the feeling aside and continued.

As I neared the bottom, I heard a sound. A door had opened. Involuntarily I looked up and saw the shadow of James coming out of Clara's room. I panicked again, as though I had no right to be going down the stairs. Perhaps I didn't, but I would never let them know.

Just the same, I hoped he hadn't seen me. I couldn't get over my feeling of guilt for being in this house. Every step made me feel more apologetic, more unsure of myself, but I made myself continue for Benjamin's sake.

At the bottom I looked up again. Once, I heard a faint sound and hoped it was James going into his own room. But it was dark and shadowy up there. I couldn't really see.

The best thing was to hurry on. I ran as quietly as I could, toward the back of the house. A cellar door would have to be somewhere in the rear. I reached the back of the stairs

And there underneath the stairs, almost hidden, way in the back, was a door. It could be a closet, but it could lead downstairs. I stepped over to it and turned the knob. It opened and at once I could feel the damp cool air of a cellar. My breath came quickly, and a little joy leaped in me. It had been so easy! I would get Benjamin's precious letters. But I could see nothing in the darkness.

I had seen a light switch on the outside wall, just beside the door, and was about to snap it on when I heard someone coming down the stairs. Quickly I stepped inside and closed the door, all but a crack, and watched.

It was James, of course. I watched as he looked up

and down the hall, then crossed to the library. He's
looking for me, I thought. As I stood watching, I heard
another door open, in the back of the house, and a man
came scuffling down the hall right past me. I guessed it
was Harry, the handyman. He had on work clothes and
carried some wood for the fireplaces.

As soon as he was out of sight, I slipped out and
snapped on the light switch. Just as I did, I saw
the library door open, and I hurriedly stepped back
inside and closed the door. James had seen me! I
went weak all over, then stiffened, angry with myself.
I was not accountable to him! As far as he knew, I had
a perfect right to be going down to the cellar. It was
my conscience that was shaking me up—and his following me, spying on me. Well, no matter; I owed him
no explanation. I listened by the door for him, but all
was quiet. Then I turned and looked down—and shivered.

There, beneath me, was a flight of the steepest stairs I
had ever seen, with steps of unbacked boards like a lad-
der and only a jerry-built banister to hold onto. In the
middle of the floor below I could see a huge furnace
and, far in the back, a row of what Benjamin had called
bins, really storage spaces. Around the side of the walls
were barrels and boxes.

The big problem for me now was to climb down those
steep stairs.

I stood for a moment, uncertain. Then I tightened my
robe around me, braced myself with a deep breath, and
started down. Very cagily, I took one step at a time. The
stairs squeaked and shook a little, but I managed to
keep going, my desire to satisfy Benjamin urging me on.

I was almost a quarter of the way down, one foot out,
feeling for the next step, when the lights went out. All at
once, I was in pitch darkness.

I stumbled, lost my balance, screamed and tumbled down. It was like falling into hell.

Then I hit the bottom and blacked out.

IT WAS SATAN who discovered me, saved me. If he hadn't been prowling around the halls, or if his sensitive ears hadn't picked up my scream—who knows what would have happened?

Susan had just left the kitchen, on her way to the dining room, when she thought she heard a scream. But James, whom she saw in the library doorway, said it must have been a gull, or one of the other birds or animals outside. He said he had just come from upstairs and all was well.

Taking his word for it, she had started back to the kitchen, when she saw Satan, his fur strangely ruffled, sniffing around the hall. When he didn't follow her (it was near his dinner time), she stood in the doorway and waited for him. But instead of coming, he turned under the stairs and started scratching at the cellar door.

She thought perhaps some wild creature had got caught down there. It had happened once before, when a delivery was made through the cellar. So she went to open the door. Satan would know. Cats sensed things and had keen hearing. Immediately he disappeared down the stairs. Then she snapped on the lights and saw me.

I learned all this later of course, after they had carried me upstairs, after I had awakened and found the doctor sitting beside me in a chair and James, Clara, Emma and Susan surrounding the bed. Only the hero, Satan, wasn't there. But the minute I could listen, Susan told me what he'd done.

James was especially solicitous. "You don't want to

tire her," he said, hovering over me and patting my head.

"You'll be fine," the doctor said as he prepared to leave. "You've got a few cuts and bruises, but nothing's broken. Very fortunate. A fall like that could have killed you if you had hit your head."

"I don't know why you went down there at all," Aunt Clara said. "You should have sent Harry for whatever you needed."

"I just...felt like rummaging," I said to excuse myself. "There were some old things I thought I might look at." I knew I shouldn't mention Benjamin's request, just as I knew that Clara was dying of curiosity.

"Don't fret now," James said in a soothing tone. "It's all over and you're safe and sound. That's the main thing."

"But the lights," I said, "they went out. That's why I fell—I lost my balance."

"It must have been a short," James said quickly.

"A short!" The doctor looked up, a little incredulous.

"Well, you know," James went on smoothly, "a broken wire—somewhere inside. It's an old house."

"But they went on again. Susan snapped them right on again." It was Emma, also incredulous.

Susan agreed, "I did, yes." Then thoughtfully, she remarked, "It could have been Harry, though he denies it. He wouldn't have known anyone was down there. And he's always being scolded for leaving the lights on. He might have snapped them off, thinking he had left them on himself."

"Of course that's it," James said with a tone of finality. "But it's all over and you're safe, so we mustn't blame him."

They started to leave then, the doctor and Emma and Susan, while Clara stood over me, smoothing my hair.

"You need a rest, child. That must have shaken you up, no matter what the doctor says. Try to get some sleep, my dear." And she kissed me before leaving with James.

They were quite a pair. Acting as though they really cared for me when not an hour ago either one of them could have cut my throat.

Well, so be it. All I wanted now was to have Andre come home. I would tell him about Benjamin and the letters, and perhaps he would get them for me. Heaven knows, I could never go down there again. Yet Benjamin was on my mind. Was he waiting for me?

I was glad when Emma came back a little while later with a cup of broth. I asked her about him.

"Is Grandfather sleeping?"

"Yes," she said, "and he's going to have to do a lot more of it. The doctor looked in on him and found him very agitated. He ordered him sedated. He said it will set him back if he doesn't keep quiet. So I have some pills for him for the next few days."

Well, that would give me time to get the letters. And perhaps it would really be better for him anyway. Surely reading them would have stirred up too much emotion for him. Better to let him rest and wait.

With that I turned over, a little painfully because of my bruises, and drifted off to sleep. Strangely, I didn't nave my usual recurring dream. I slept deeply, peacefully for a while.

Later, in the deep of the night, I heard myself calling, "Mother, mother!"

Still half-asleep, I seemed to be opening the closet door in Clara's room as I had done earlier that day. And then I saw clearly the face of the woman in the painting.

Such a beautiful face, with her deep eyes and dark hair. I knew instinctively that it was Roma's mother, as one always knows the truth in the dead of night.

But why was she hidden away in the closet?

For no reason I began to cry quietly, like a child. The tears were wet on my face when I drifted off to sleep again.

CHAPTER TWELVE

A PING from the little white phone on my bedside table awakened me. For three days I had seen that phone and never expected it to ring. Who could be calling me? It was with trepidation that I lifted the receiver and breathed a cautious hello.

"Is that you, Roma?"

André's voice was unmistakable. I sat up. "Where are you?"

"I'm here. In Boston."

"In Boston!" My heart twisted into a knot. "You mean you're not home yet?"

"I couldn't help it. I have important business. I have another appointment this afternoon."

"But you can't leave me here alone another day! I can't—"

"Roma!"

His warning tone reminded me it would be unwise to talk too freely over the phone. Then he went on, a little tensely, "Emma told me you had an accident yesterday."

"Yes," I said with a touch of self-pity, "I'm full of scrapes and bruises, and I think my shoulder is wrenched."

"What in God's name were you doing on the cellar stairs?" He said it in exasperation, between his teeth, cutting me off cold.

I froze. He didn't care about me, I thought. I was just

someone he was using. I remained silent, determined not to speak until he did.

Finally he must have sensed my hurt.

"Roma," he said more softly, "I'm sorry about your fall. Be careful, dear. Take...care."

I was a little mollified, but not enough.

"I will," I said. "Goodbye now." Then I hung up.

I knew it was a horrid thing to do, but my frustration had reached its limits. I was nervous and angry and outraged. Here he had forced me into this trap and then walked off and left me. He had promised to help me and protect me. And what did he do? Go to Boston and leave me here alone to fight a wildcat, a shrew, and a rejected lover! Worse, to be almost killed. Yes, I knew it was James who had snapped off the lights.

I flung the covers off me, jumped out of bed and ran to the dressing room, where I splashed my face with cold water. One thing was certain: I was not going to remain in this room all day waiting for André. I had to get out. I had to see the ocean.

I was brushing my hair when Emma came in. She seemed surprised to see me up, but I assured her I felt fine and inquired about Grandfather Benjamin.

"He has to be kept very quiet. Doctor's orders. No visitors today. Shall I bring up your breakfast, ma'am?"

"No thank you, Emma. I'm not at all hungry."

Emma left then, and a great surge of excitement went through me as I rushed to Roma's closet to find warm clothes. It was already April, but it was still cold. Quickly, with impatient hands, I pushed back the sliding doors and found what I needed: a warm camelhair coat and pants to match, a sweater, a pair of flat, rubber-soled shoes and a bright flowered scarf to protect me from the wind. I got dressed and quickly tied the scarf around my head. I was ready.

Suddenly I remembered that we were high on a cliff and that the ocean, though so close, was far below us. How would I get down?

I ran to the French windows, opened them and stepped out onto the little balcony, searching the ground beneath the house. It was the first time I had ever looked straight down; before, I had always looked out to sea. I saw greenery: spruces, clumps of bushes and great twisted pine trees, some of them leaning to one side. They were quite a sight in themselves. And then, over at the right, I saw a narrow row of steps leading straight down to the ocean. I turned then and left the room.

No one was about. Stealthily, I tiptoed down the stairs. I was only ten steps from the bottom, when I had the sensation of falling. I gripped the banister. Had I tripped? No, not really. But a dizzy sense of tumbling head over heels swept through me. I stood still, trying to overcome the queer feeling of "seeing" myself fall down the stairs, hitting the last one with my head. So vivid was it, so real, that my hand automatically flew up to protect me. After a second it passed and I moved on, but more slowly, more cautiously. And then I ran out the front door.

I couldn't believe the excitement that tore through me just from the smell of the air! I was filled with elation as I breathed that wonderful mixture of scents: grass and pine, combined with the smell of the ocean. My very soul leaped up to drink it all in.

For a moment I stopped to look back at the house where I had been imprisoned for the past few days. It was a beauty, squarely facing the ocean. Made of white clapboard, with long Greek columns for support, it was even larger than I had imagined. All the windows had deep-green storm shutters, and all the upstairs rooms had balconies. Downstairs, I recognized the great picture window of the library. Many spruces tucked close to the foundation lent it an aura of luxury. The steps to the front door, which had graceful iron railings on each side, curved inward toward the top, and fanned out at the bottom.

I stood for a moment just looking, transfixed. Home, I thought. Roma's home. And then I gulped, a lump in my throat, an ache in my heart. I turned from the house as my elation became longing and started toward the ocean.

The steps were very steep. I had to pick my way carefully, grateful for the rubber soles of my shoes. Finally I was down. Oh, the feeling of infinity, of a different kind of "home." Through and under all the noises—the thundering boom and splashing spray of the ocean as it hit the rocks; the steady, slower-paced rhythm of the waves and the softly lisping edges of the sea as it touched the sand, the gulls screaming; even the buoy clanging in the distance—peace and a kind of wonder filled my heart. Tightening the scarf around my head against the wind, I walked along, and the air seemed to breathe my soul back into me.

I must have walked a mile or so along the beach and back. Near the house was a long stretch of rocks that formed a jetty out into the sea. I knew I had to go out there. The very rocks themselves, wet and strong and timeless, called me, gave me strength. I managed very well, jumping from one to the other, feeling closer and closer to the cold invigorating sea. Finally I sat down on one of the rocks to think, to sort things out.

Now that I was out of the house, I could feel *myself* once more. Not Roma Starr, but the girl who, for want of a name of her own, called herself Sara Smith. The house had cast a spell on me. Up there I was beginning

to believe that Benjamin Starr really was my grandfather and that I had a right to be with him. I believed
that I had to protect him from Clara and James. André
had told me that they were predators, and my experience of yesterday proved it. If they knew of
Roma's death, I knew they would tell Benjamin about
it so that he would die of shock and a broken heart,
and they would inherit his fortune. I had to prevent
that. It was my *raison d'être*. I was needed; Benjamin
needed me!

Now, out here in the strong pure air, it all seemed a
little unreal. What was real was that I was alone, that I
had an unknown future to face. A kind of thrill mixed
with fear ran through me. What would I do when André
brought back my ring and when Benjamin was well
enough for me to be on my way? Which way would I
go? Where?

But there were no answers. My mind was a blank. I
closed my eyes for a moment, and there rose before me
the vision of my ring. The laughing face seemed to be
still this time, but larger than life and waiting. Waiting
for what? I opened my eyes to try to dispel the face that
had invaded my peace so many times in the past year.

It was then that I heard a voice calling, "Roma!
Roma!" It seemed to come from very far off, and for a
moment I had difficulty adjusting to the present, to
where I was.

I turned my head toward shore and saw James waving
madly as he began to climb the rocks and start toward
me. Everything in me shriveled. Good God! I didn't
want to see him! After yesterday what did we have to
say to each other? I didn't trust him and apparently he
hated me. Or perhaps it was love-hate. Both could be
dangerous. Yet, based on his performance after the
cellar episode, I knew he was going to act as though

nothing had happened, as though we were the best of friends. Very slick.

And now he was fast approaching me, hopping and jumping along the wet rocks. I was trapped.

"What the heck are you doing way out here? You know it's dangerous." He was panting as he sat down beside me. "But that's what you like, isn't it? Danger."

I didn't like the way he said it; there was more to it than I understood. But I tried not to show it. I had felt perfectly safe; the rocks were high and firm, and the air filled me with courage, but now I was nervous. *He* had made me nervous. I didn't want to talk to him. But there was no escape. He settled himself close to me—too close.

"What are you trying to do, run away from me?" He playfully tucked his arm around me

Gently, carefully, I removed it. "Please," I reminded him, "you *know* I'm married now."

At that he broke out into a great hollow laugh. "Oh, Roma, you incredible creature! Don't tell me you've become a puritan! You can't have changed that much!"

I was silent. I didn't know how I was going to steer the conversation into something less personal. But I tried.

"Does this place look the same to you after all the years you've been away?"

"All the years! You make it sound like a hundred." He cozied up to me again and tried to make his eyes catch mine. I averted my gaze as I babbled, "I've heard it said that nothing remains the same. Everything is changing all the time, especially the shoreline and the sea."

"Don't get philosophical with me. I didn't come out here for that." He turned full toward me, confronting me. "Roma! I want you to be *yourself* with me! Please!"

He was frantically trying to reach me—and I was trying just as frantically to escape.

"You owe me some explanation," he went on, "you can't deny that. You *did* love me. And you *did* make me a promise. We were to live here together. I dreamed all these years about coming home to you and to this place. I counted on it. Mother and I, we both did. You know that. But you cheated us—you cheated us for that arrogant, phony, fortune-hunting beach bum! How could you do it, Roma? How could you! You promised me!"

He grabbed my arm again and I could feel his mounting tension. Frightened, I struck out wildly with the only thing I could think of:

"I was only sixteen. You can't hold me to what I said then. I was only a child."

"You haven't been a child since you were twelve. Don't forget, I *know* you. Whatever you are, whatever you've been, you belong to me. We belong together, you know that. That's why you made me swear that last day that I'd come back here for you. But you broke your promise, Roma. Why?"

This was too much. I stood up. I had to be free of him, but he stood up too and barred my way. So I turned and went further out on the rocks. He followed me, grabbed my arm again and spun me toward him.

"Roma, damn it! Don't try to run away from me. I've got to say it—I can't forgive you. You played around with me and I hate you for it. Ever since I went away, and all through the war with ships going down under me, it was you I saw, you I loved, you I stayed alive for. . .and then, God help me, just at the end when I would have been coming home to you. . .that letter. . . that unforgiveable letter of yours! I swore I'd kill you if I ever saw you again!"

He started to shake me. "Why did you do it, Roma? Why?"

My teeth chattering, frightened, I tried again to pull away but he yanked me back, screaming "Why, why?"

As he spoke his handsome, ingenuous face seemed to change to a stony masklike hardness that terrified me. I made a tremendous effort and twisted lose from him. As I did I stepped back and something wobbled beneath my foot and over I went...down, down into the icy water beneath.

Of course I screamed, tried to clutch the slippery rock. Incredibly, there was no bottom that my foot could touch! Water was swirling around me like a whirlpool, pulling me down and preventing me from getting a hold on the rocks. I was frightened as I had never been before.

"Help!" I screamed, gulping water as it threatened to cover my head. "Help me!" In that instant, looking up, I had a water-blurred vision of James's face looking down at me from the top of the rocks. It was still mask like and frozen. *He* seemed frozen. I had the horrified feeling that he was going to let me drown.

"James," I cried, "help me! There's no bottom.... I'm going under!"

Then suddenly there was only dark, tumultuous confusion. A great wave must have swallowed me up, first dashing me against the rocks, then pushing me away so that there was nothing but water. I knew I was drowning. Frantically, I tried to tread water, and for a second I managed to get my head far enough out of the water to breathe. In that second I seemed to hear voices shouting and a great deal of splashing. But everything was far off and dreamlike. It was a useless struggle against the great icy waves. What seemed like years later, I was gripped by a strong arm, and I was pulled along through the raging waves. Finally I felt water draining away from my heavy clothes. Someone was carrying me in his arms, walking on solid ground, stumbling, then stretching me out on the sand on my stomach, my head to one side. Half opening my eyes, I saw James, dripping wet, panting, leaning over me, frantically loosening my clothes and whispering hoarsely, "Roma! My God. Roma. you're all right, aren't you?"

He had come through at the last minute! I closed my eyes. Then suddenly there seemed to be people running down the beach. Vaguely, as in a dream, I heard them, felt them crowding around. There was Aunt Clara, of course, ordering everyone to stand back. Her voice cut through to me, and I opened my eyes again and saw her and Susan and Harry and André.... André? Where had he come from?

Then his voice blasted my eardrums. "What have you done to her, for God's sake?" And he knelt, pushing James aside, and began to pump my sides.

And that was all. I suppose I was in shock. The last thing I remember was André's lifting me, and my feeling heavy, very heavy.

CHAPTER THIRTEEN

THE NEXT TIME I heard voices, they were feminine. I immediately recognized Emma's soothing tones ("You'll be all right, dear, you just need some warmth") as she rubbed me with a fluffy towel and tucked me once again between the sheets of Roma's bed. The other voice was Clara's, clarion clear, high-pitched as ever, complaining about me as though I weren't there.

"She *knows* better than to go out on those rocks. That was deliberate recklessness. They were both forbidden as children to go running about on them. They are dangerous—there's a deep drop just a few feet from shore. And for her to go out there and risk her life—"

Something stopped her in midsentence, and I opened my eyes a slit to see what it was. It was André, coming through the door. He looked more dour than ever, and I knew, of course, that he was blaming me for having almost drowned, for having left the room at all. His mouth was drawn, and even the warm plum color of his smoking jacket had no power to put color into his face. His eyes seemed hard and bright, a little desperate, as he glanced toward me.

It was Clara who broke the silence. "Well," she said, "all's well that ends well. But all I can say is that it was a good thing that James was there—no one else would have made it. It's high tide, you know, and going out."

I was a little astonished. She was proud that it was James, not André, who had carried me out. But André ignored the remark.

"Susan is fixing some clam chowder for us all," he said. "I think we need it. I'll have mine up here with Roma."

"*I* don't need it," Clara said with a kind of personal pride. "I've had a proper breakfast. I'll go down and sit with Benjamin."

Instantly André was alert. "I wouldn't trouble him with what just happened, Clara. He mustn't be upset."

I could feel her bristling. "Why—don't you think I have a little common sense? Of course..."

Emma interrupted. "As a matter of fact, I have to bathe Mr. Benjamin and give him his medicine right away. I was just about to begin when all this happened."

"Then you'd better go ahead, Emma. I'll take care of anything my wife needs."

My wife! Those words pierced me, aroused in me a commingling of feelings I would never be able to sort out.

The room emptied, and André and I were left alone. He stood by my bed, looking down at me.

"God!" he said immediately after the door was shut. "You gave me a scare!"

I put out my hand, and he sat down on the bed beside me. "I'm sorry," I whispered, the same old weak apology that always seemed to enrage him.

But for some reason, it didn't this time. He clasped both hands over mine and said, "Thank God, I got here in time!"

Then I remembered he had said he wouldn't be home till evening. "How did you get here so soon? I didn't—"

"I canceled my appointment. I just felt I had to get home to you in a hurry."

A tide of warmth rose in me.

"You could have drowned!" he whispered. "Do you realize that? He was letting you drown! I saw him standing there. I had just driven up—God knows what made me look down that way. You can't *wait* when someone is in that water. He was *letting you drown* until he saw me running...."

His voice was full of genuine emotion, and for the moment that meant more to me than anything else. More, even, than being safe again. I looked up at him with tears in my eyes, for the first time with pure gratitude.

Then he went on, "What were you doing out on the rocks anyway? Was it James's idea?"

"No. He followed me."

"With a purpose, no doubt. Tell me—did he push you off?"

"No, he didn't. But... I think... he wanted to."

And I told him about yesterday. About my outburst to Clara and how they had both reacted—and, of course, about the cellar stairs.

He listened in a quiet rage. I could feel his anger rising. Finally, he jumped up, his fists clenched so hard that his knuckles showed white.

"By God, he really does mean to kill you!"

"He frightens me now, in a way. In another way, I feel sorry for him—"

"Sorry for him!" he exploded, interrupting me. "Good God, girl, don't be a fool! Why should you feel sorry for him? Damn emotionalism, that's what you feel. He means no good to you; you better understand it. And Clara—she probably put him up to it. I warned you of what they were like. Predators, that's what they are, predators. You've got to beware. I told you before, the safest place for you is right here, in your own room. Stay here. And stay close to me. Promise me.''

I promised, gratefully. And added, ''Then *you* must promise me. . ''

But before I could finish, Susan knocked on the door and walked in rolling a teacart. André placed a folding tray over my lap, then filled it with a deep bowl, a dish of oysterettes, and another of thick, hot, buttered tea biscuits.

André said he would eat from the cart, which held, aside from his bowl and crackers, a huge tureen of chowder. I never knew till the lid was lifted and the aroma reached my nostrils how euphoric the smell of clams could make one. In fact, I had never before tasted clams or clam chowder, but I could barely wait until Susan filled the ladle and poured the hot liquid, all creamy and buttery, into my bowl.

''I'll take my own, Susan,'' André was saying. ''Thank you. It smells delicious.''

As Susan left, she looked at me in a curious way, I thought, and then suddenly broke out in a charming smile. She was very young and healthy looking, pink cheeked and vigorous. For a second I envied her. Such a simple, uncomplicated life! And then, I remembered that a few weeks ago *I* too had had a simple, uncompli- cated life—and had run away from it!

''Come,'' André urged, ''it's no good if it gets luke- warm. You've got to eat it while it's piping hot.''

He sat down close to my bed and then broke some crackers into his bowl of chowder. I followed suit, and we both ate quietly for a few minutes. I could feel my strength coming back to me. This was heaven, I thought, and let out a little sigh of pleasure.

André looked up at me after a while and broke into a

broad smile. It was the first time I had seen him smile in a happy, contented sort of way. It changed his whole personality, as a day can change from dark and foreboding to bright and cheery. For a few moments I saw a different man. Then, as we were finishing our chowder, eating less ravenously, he broke the spell.

"And now—tell me what I must promise you."

"Not to leave me here alone again."

"I won't—after tomorrow. I have to go back—"

"But I can't be left here alone with James!"

"Just once more. I must go. Stay in this room, as I told you. You'll be safe. You've been warned."

"Not of everything." I was growing bitter

"What do you mean—not of everything?"

Then I blurted out, "You never told me that James and Roma had been...lovers."

I saw him blanch. "I...didn't know. She never told *me*. Is that what he says?"

"He pounced on me the minute he was alone with me. He berated me, Roma, for marrying you. He said I, Roma, had made a promise. He made it clear we had been...intimate."

André sat in stunned silence, as if he had suddenly been struck dumb. But once I had started talking I couldn't stop.

"But you can imagine what I went through. He says I'm nothing like the Roma he said goodbye to. He says my personality has changed. He blames you for it now, but he feels something *different* about me. I'm frightened."

"It's true—you are very different."

"Then how can you leave me here with him?"

He placed his hand tightly over mine. "I don't want to, but I have to. Just once more. It's for Benjamin and...for you. Try to stay away from James. Stay in here.''

"But he won't leave me alone. He hates me now. And he hates you. He says you have no right to be here. He says he and Clara, not you, belong here with Roma." I said it bitterly, accusingly, because I was frightened.

I waited while he stared at me. Then, when he said nothing, I went on, "He called you a beach bum—some man Roma had met on a beach. He says you're a fortune hunter."

I watched him grinding his teeth, but still he said nothing.

"André! You owe me some explanation! Say something!"

"All right, all right! Damn James! I might have expected that of him if I had known they were lovers. But I didn't. She never even mentioned him to me until Benjamin wanted us to wait until James returned from the Pacific so we could invite him and Clara to the wedding."

I could tell he was deeply upset. "And then?"

"Then she told me what I have already told you about them, and that she didn't want to see them. It was after that she suggested we run down to Connecticut and be married. And we did."

"How long had you known her?"

"Less than a week."

"And did she pick you up on a beach? Were you...a beach bum?"

He smiled a faint, sardonic little twist of a smile. Somehow, it annoyed me. Then, remembering how skeptical I had been of him in the beginning, I said, "Was he right about you? Are you...a fortune hunter?"

I saw the color rise in his pale face, and I was immediately sorry I had said it. For even if he was, would he be likely to say so?

He pushed the teacart away, slapped his napkin down, and stood up. When he spoke, his voice was low and trembling with suppressed rage.

"My dear, you are going to have to decide that for yourself." And he turned abruptly and started for the door.

I threw the covers off and ran after him, making him face me. "How can I decide when you don't tell me anything? You expect me to have blind faith in you!"

"Yes," he snapped back, "I guess I do. But then," he said, staring at me, his agate eyes penetrating me, "I keep forgetting—you know nothing about me."

We remained facing each other, breathing hard.

After a minute his eyes clouded over, and he turned away. "I'm sorry," he said bitterly, almost sarcastically, "of course I shouldn't expect you to have faith in me. I'm a stranger to you."

For some reason it was as though he had slapped me. The tears gushed to my eyes. What had I done?

He continued in a cold, businesslike tone. "Very well. I'll tell you. Roma and I did meet on a beach. I had been sleeping there. Call it being a beach bum if you like. I couldn't paint anymore. I had to be down by the sea. I used to feel her there."

Unseeing, he walked past me to the window, and I knew he was speaking of his Sybil.

"I used to dream that she would appear, that she would come running up the beach toward me, arms outstretched. I dreamed that dream over and over. And then one morning I half woke, and I actually thought I saw her. I rushed to her, overpowered her with my pent-up emotions—and, well, of course it wasn't Sybil. It was Roma. It was a bad scene. But she understood that I was troubled and forgave what must have seemed like a madman's attack, and just took over my life And so we were married, as I told you, within the week. That was a year ago. We came back here then, to stay with Benjamin. He had had a slight stroke—from all the excitement, I suppose—and it wasn't until he recovered completely that we felt free to go on a belated honeymoon. That was just a few weeks ago. That was when you met Roma. . . and lost her.''

Here he turned back to me abruptly, his temper rising as he went on, ''So now you have the whole story. I didn't know much about Roma when we married. I didn't know she had all that money, or even that her stepbrother was in love with her. By the same token, she didn't know much about me. But Roma was a reckless girl. She took chances. She took a chance on me.''

He flung the last sentence at me in an aggrieved manner and left.

I stood there feeling lost, alone. After a minute, under my breath, I cried, ''Oh, André!''

It was a cry of longing and pain. He was so unreachable, so difficult. I had only wanted to understand a little more. I thought I had a right to know. But somehow he always put me in the wrong, made me feel guilty. For what?

And yet something in me ached for him. For some unexplained reason I identified with him and with his vague suffering to the point where I felt a wave of unreality. I was in over my head, feeling things I could not understand, wanting to love and be loved by a man I could never reach—a man, who, I couldn't stop remembering, loved another, a ghost who would always stand between us as she had stood between him and Roma

But wasn't I, in my own way, a ghost? I, who could

remember nothing, who would have nothing to give to this man to fill his emptiness.

I had to push aside all this feeling I had for him. It weakened and confused me. It would be too painful to love a man so fierce and steadfast, a man who could love only once, and forever.

CHAPTER FOURTEEN

LATE THAT AFTERNOON, long after André had left me, James came in to see me. I was sitting in the chair by the window. He looked rather sheepish as he came toward me all wrapped up in a long white terry robe. He apparently had not dressed after his dousing in the ocean.

"Have you caught a cold?" I asked, determined to be natural, even casual, with him.

"Who, me?" He laughed at the absurdity. "If you'd been knocked overboard as many times as I have, you'd know I was immune."

I could see he was going to be as casual as I was. "You all right now?" he asked cheerfully as he seated himself on the edge of my hassock.

"I think so," I answered cautiously. "It was foolish of me to go out there and cause so much trouble."

"Not really. Remember what I always used to say— anything, anytime—for Roma."

He smiled at me, a little pleadingly, I thought. And for a moment I had a flicker of sympathy for him, talking to a girl he only *thought* he knew. A wave of guilt swept through me.

"I'm glad you're all right," he went on, "because I have a suggestion to make. Do you think you could come down to dinner tonight?"

I felt a little shiver of fear. Down to dinner, face to face with Aunt Clara, and nowhere to run?

He went on, "I came in to tell you—she feels hurt about your not remembering her birthday."

Her birthday! Of course I had no idea it was her birthday.

"She's awfully sentimental, though it's the last thing she'd admit. And you've never forgotten her birthday, not one single year, until now. I told her it was because you'd had an accident and been sick and all—you probably didn't even know what day it is."

How true that was! But I had to try to answer him. "Oh, James, I really don't. I hardly know what month it is!"

"Well, it's her birthday—the sixth of April—and I wish you hadn't forgotten. She thinks you've changed awfully. And she feels neglected. You know you haven't had a really good visit with her since she arrived."

I had to make up my mind quickly. It would be dreadful to refuse to go down to dinner, especially since I had appeared well enough to go out on the rocks.

"Of course I'll come down." I said it quickly so as not to realize the extent of my fear.

"Good!" He seemed delighted. "I knew you'd be a good sport. Now, what I thought was, we'd make it a formal party. Mother loves dressing up and all that sort of thing, remember? Susan can get a local girl in to help, and Harry can serve. It'll be great fun having a party again. We can dress and have cocktails and music at seven, then go in to a sit-down dinner at eight. Mother would love that. And it will make her feel better if I tell her it was your idea. You know, pretend you hadn't really forgotten after all."

He had it all planned so neatly. I couldn't help wondering if the party wasn't for himself as well as for his mother. But suddenly, it seemed rather exciting. Hazardous, like the rocks, but exciting.

"Is it all right then?" he asked, standing up and ready to go. "I'll set everything up with Susan. You won't have to worry about a thing. Just dress like a princess and come down. Will you tell André or shall I?"

The thought of telling André unnerved me. "You tell him it's all planned."

"I hope he doesn't bite my head off. He acted as though I was going to let you drown!"

"Of course you weren't!" I said quickly, although, remembering his face looking down at me over the rocks, I wasn't so sure.

As soon as he was gone, I got up. I was nervous but excited, too, about what I had promised to do. After all, it sounded like a little fun and I needed some kind of activity to get me out of the room. I had had enough. For the moment, the dinner party seemed safer than the ocean and the rocks. Or was it?

I had gone to the closet to try to choose a gown from Roma's wardrobe when Emma came in. She was surprised to see me up.

"My! You do bounce back, ma'am. I came to see how you are."

"I'm fine, Emma. You take such good care of me. And we're having a party for Mrs. Starr tonight. It's her birthday."

"Oh," she said, "that's nice. I hope you keep warm, though."

Then I remembered Benjamin. "Do you think it will disturb Grandfather—having a party?"

"Oh, no, he sleeps soundly. I think he'd want you to have it."

"Would you like to come to the party?"

"Oh, thank you. Perhaps I'll look in. But I don't like to leave him alone for long. Anything could happen, you know. Sometimes in just a minute."

That gave me a twinge, made me realize how tenuous the life of dear old Benjamin was. What would I do if he passed away? And what, indeed, would I continue to do if he did not? A rush of uncertainty, almost agony, shot through me as I realized in vivid terms all over again my untenable position. I think I let Emma leave without speaking to her, and when André came through the door a few moments later, my nerves were stretched taut like wire, my momentary childlike pleasure in a supper party spoiled.

He came toward me and, as usual, spoke irritably. "What is James talking about? Don't tell me you've really agreed to go down to this party of his."

I was in no mood to endure any criticism. I nodded. "I'm going to do... what I feel like doing."

"I should think you'd have had enough of that after this morning."

"I've had enough of all of it," I said, and then added, to my own amazement, "I can't go on with this."

He immediately softened. "Yes, you can. For Benjamin. For your grandfather."

"He's not my grandfather, as you well know." And then, I said, "That's the trouble. I wish he were."

"Then help him! Don't do anything that might kill him. Hold on!"

Those words again! *Trust me! Hold on!*

"But I can't hold on with the two of them here. My nerves are cracking."

"Tell me—what happened yesterday with Clara?"

I told him about Satan flying at her and scratching her. "And she ended by blaming me and demanding that I get rid of him."

"You can't do that! Roma would never do that!"

"I said Satan would stay."

"Good girl."

"But I'm scared. I know she'll find out."

"Then why did you agree just now to go downstairs to dinner? I try to help you, to protect you, but you deliberately keep running into trouble."

I realized what he said was true, but I couldn't seem to help myself. I was nervous and close to tears. "I. . .I thought I *ought* to go. How would it look? What excuse could I offer? Besides, I'm tired of being cooped up. I'm—I'm—"

"Listen to me," he said, placing his hands on my shoulders and speaking in a placating tone, "I've been to Boston trying to find out how best to handle. . .our situation. I've been seeing doctors, several of them. And I'm going to bring back a specialist if I can."

I felt a sense of relief as he spoke. Why hadn't he told me what he was doing? I felt better about him.

"Please, don't crack up now," he was saying, "I'm trying my best."

"Well—what shall I do about dinner tonight?"

"You've already promised, so I guess you'll have to go through with it." He suddenly smiled at me. "I know—give her a present! That will help heal the wounds."

"But what? I haven't anything."

"I know just the thing."

He went into the dressing room and after a minute came back out, holding a gold medallion on a chain. It was as large as a silver dollar, and in its center were colored stones—beautiful blues and greens and reds.

"It's a reproduction of a stained glass window in the Cathedral of Chartres. Roma told me once how Clara coveted it and that she intended to give it to her someday. Why not give it to her now?"

He dangled the medallion before me. It was an unusual thing, surely one of a kind. And yet, I felt I had seen

it before. And then I knew. It was around the neck of
the woman in the painting—the one I had seen in the
closet.

"Whose was it?" I asked.

"I told you. Roma's. Why?"

"There's a painting of a woman in the closet of the
room that Clara's in. There's a medallion like this one
around her neck. I saw it."

"I've never seen the painting," he said.

Then, thinking of my conversation with Benjamin, I
asked abruptly, "What happened to Roma's mother?
Her real mother, I mean."

He didn't answer me at once. Then he said, "I don't
know. She never told me."

"Didn't you ask her?"

"Yes. I did once. She said no one ever spoke about
her in this house. Grandfather forbade it."

"That's strange, don't you think?"

"She said one day she'd tell me what she knew, anyway. But she never did."

"The painting is of her mother," I said.

"How do you know?"

"I just know. There was something familiar about
her. I couldn't forget her. And then I had a dream. I
saw her face. I must have been dreaming I was Roma,
and I was calling, Mother, Mother!"

He was silent for a moment. Then he seemed to want
to change the subject.

"Well, what shall we do? Give the medallion to Clara
or not?"

"You said Roma meant to give it to her. I guess it
would be fitting."

"All right. I'll have Susan wrap it. Now come and
we'll choose a gown for you. You know James has de-
creed that we dress. It will be a nice change for you, I

guess. Just stay close to me, and I'll try to protect you."

I followed him into the dressing room, where he was already rolling back the wardrobe doors. He skimmed his hand along a row of long gowns, passing over all the brightly colored and finally bringing out a white chiffon gown with a deep oval neckline adorned with a self-ruffle. The skirt flared in a full circle.

"You know," he said, "Roma had two sides to her. I learned that very quickly. This dress represents her angelic side. Wear it. It suits you." And he flung it over the back of the chair as though that settled it.

He moved then back to a mahogany jewel box. "You'll need some jewelry."

I watched as he fingered an array of jewels; then, out of a small top compartment, he lifted an emerald ring. He turned to me quickly, holding it out.

"Let's see if it fits."

When he lifted my hand and began to slip it on my finger, the queer, indescribable feeling came over me. This ring was not *my* emerald ring, of course. No mocking satyr's face looked up at me, no golden hands unwound to beckon to me; it was a simple gold ring with a large square-cut stone. And yet, it was as though I were participating in a scene from an unfamiliar play. I struggled not to reveal the wave of unreality that had flooded over me. I could not have described it if I tried, for it was combined with a kind of eerie remembrance of things past. I say "eerie" because there was no trace of true remembrance—only a sickening feeling of... of... something.

I pulled my hand away and took off the ring. "I can't wear it," I said. "I... don't want to wear any jewelry."

"What's the matter?" He looked at me searchingly, too close for comfort. "You've turned white."

I moved away from him, going out into the bedroom

and sitting on the edge of the bed. I heard him replace the ring and close the box. Then he came to me.

"You're right. You don't need any jewelry," he said. "Just your beautiful self."

It was a nice compliment and, I thought, understanding. He didn't press me for what had happened, but just stood by, waiting. Slowly the feeling passed, and I said what was uppermost in my mind.

"Have you found my flight bag? Did you bring it back with you?"

He hesitated just a second. "Oh, I meant to tell you. You needn't worry about that. It's safe."

"Have you got it then?" My breath came quickly.

"Well—I didn't have time this morning. But it's being held for you. It's safe. You'll have it."

A weight seemed to be lifted from me. It was as though a little knot of fear inside me had been loosened.

"But I want it. I want it with me. Can't you get it?"

"Of course. But I've been busy. And then I hurried home this morning."

"But you will bring it next time, won't you?"

"I will bring it to you soon, never fear." He said it softly, tenderly, as though he were concerned for me. And then he leaned down and kissed my brow and left quickly.

I stood in the room alone, very still. The thought of the return of my ring had done something for me, catapulted me back to the days at the hospital when my ring goaded me daily into some sort of action until at last I had taken the dangerous plunge that had landed me here, in a little town in a far-off country. Here, where I was kept a virtual prisoner by a strange man, where I loved an old man and pretended to be somebody I was not. Was this what my ring, with its beckoning fingers and mocking laugh, had promised?

I moved slowly toward the windows, pulled the curtains aside, and looked out at the raging sea bursting against the rocks. I let my eyes drift beyond the violent surf to the wide, calm horizon in the far, far distance. I knew then that I was beginning to love this place, that it was taking hold of me, and that when the moment came to leave, it would be wrenching to my soul.

And yet, even in that moment, something was stirring in me. The old agony was creeping in. I knew that when André brought my ring back and I slipped it on my finger, as I had sworn to do, I would be overcome by the same nagging questions: where did it come from? Who had put it on my finger? Who was I? The nightmares would follow. The satyr would grin up at me and mock and lure and tantalize, and there would be no peace. No peace, until he gave up his secret.

Abruptly, almost angrily, I turned from the window. Very well. I knew what was coming. But for tonight, just for tonight, I would be Roma Starr. I would play the game and enjoy it; I would believe I had a home and a grandfather here, in this beautiful place. Tonight I would be mistress of Starr Mansion and forget the satyr ring. It could wait. It could all wait—until tomorrow.

CHAPTER FIFTEEN

IT WAS AMAZING what my change of attitude did for me. My heart was suddenly light, my step firm. It was as though a sleeping woman whom I hadn't known existed had been awakened in me.

At once I began to prepare for the party that evening, as other women had prepared for other parties many times before. For me, it was the first such occasion. And yet I went about it with the ease of long experience, as though the knowledge of this lay submerged in me just beneath the surface.

To begin with I soaked rapturously in the pale pink sunken tub, pouring in enormous amounts of perfumed oil. Later, wrapped in a terry robe, I sat before the dressing table, gazing at all the tools of beauty. There were oils and powders and makeup bases, lipsticks and eyebrow pencils and mascara and shadows. And of course nail polishes, every variety and color.

I used the makeup sparingly and surprisingly skillfully so that by the time I finished, I seemed to be looking at a stranger. The girl who had left the hospital in London was but a dull copy. I looked without vanity but with a kind of impersonal wonder at the radiant, glowing face framed by a wealth of golden hair.

Who was this girl? Then I smiled, pleased. Perhaps for the first time I really would feel like Roma—Roma, who had driven a car a hundred miles an hour, who had had James as a lover, who had married André.

The important thing now was my dress, still over the back of the chair where André had tossed it. Looking at it now, I had a change of heart. Why shouldn't I choose my own dress, something that suited my mood, my personality, better than that? Angelic, he had said! Indeed! Would an angel be in my position tonight? No, I wanted something vital and exciting.

I ran to the closet and began to look through the gowns. A red satin caught my eye. I pulled it out; it was straight, slim, strapless. I held it up against me, hesitated, then decided no. I wanted something...something... Ah, there it was: an emerald green mat jersey, designed like a Greek goddess's robe—long, flowing, and draped over one shoulder, leaving the other bare. Did I dare wear this? I hesitated. Then I decided, why not? If Roma could, why couldn't I?

I slipped into it and felt a marvelous change come over me. Suddenly I was free, elated. Like a Bacchante I danced into the bedroom in my bare feet—wild, carefree and happy. Perhaps as Roma used to be. Perhaps even as I had felt once myself. Somewhere, sometime.

Exhilarated, I continued twirling until I heard a strange low growling sound coming from the dressing room. Of course, it was Satan. I spotted him peeking around the corner, staring at me as if I had gone mad.

"Satan!" I said bravely in my new mood. "What is the matter with you? I have a right to dance."

He came out skittishly then, on tiptoe, and tore around the room himself, as though he were showing me that he could do it better than I. And indeed he could. He leaped into the air every few feet, then up and over the bed and around again. Finally he went to the door and scratched at it until I opened it for him.

He was gone in a flash. I watched him almost fly down the stairs, leaping five or six at a time, barely touching his feet to them. For the first time I appreciated his wildness and his grace. It passed through my mind that, given a while, I might even grow to feel about him the way Roma had.

When he was out of sight I stood for a moment in the doorway. The aromas of delicious foods floated up from the kitchen and I could hear people hurrying back and forth in a flurry of preparation. It gave the house an air of excitement. By now I too was excited.

I closed the door. I had to finish dressing. Quickly I found some dainty green sandals for my feet and then took a last glance at myself in the mirror.

As soon as I looked, I knew my hair was all wrong. I couldn't wear my hair forward, so sweetly around my face. Not with this dress. Defiantly, I took hold of the brush and swept my hair up, pulling it away from my face and twisting it into a Grecian knot at the back of my head.

Perfect! Surely Roma would have done the same. Only now, my new hairdo demanded earrings. Hurriedly, I opened Roma's elaborate jewel box and looked through the little drawers. No earrings. Could it be that Roma never wore earrings? In my amazement I began to look elsewhere. I opened one of the top drawers in her dressing table, and there beneath my startled eyes were piles of jewels. Not expensive, genuine pieces like those in her jewel box, but costume jewelry, large and flamboyant—things a Gypsy might wear.

I took a deep breath. This was a surprise. I suppose it represented the side of Roma I could not have known. There would have to be—yes, there was—a pair of large hoops, just what I needed. Pure glass, of course, but exciting. I stood before the mirror in my new smooth, pulled-back hairstyle and clipped them on. Yes. Some female sense told me that they were just right. Satisfied, I decided it was time to go down.

As I came out of the dressing room, I became aware of a change in the atmosphere. It penetrated the walls of the room with something like an electric charge. I hurried to the window and saw a wild foreboding dark sea with breathtaking whitecaps and a sky of black threatening clouds that seemed so low I could touch them. I had never been afraid of storms, but suddenly I felt as though the world were coming to an end. It made me want to join the others quickly.

I rushed to the door, and just as I opened it, the suspended violence broke loose. I heard the distant threatening rumble rise to a drumlike crescendo and burst in a crash that froze me where I stood. I gripped the doorknob. I wanted to return to the safety of my room, but I couldn't move. The terrible wildness in the air completely unnerved me. I had never experienced anything quite like it . . . except . . . except . . . And here a shadowy memory took over—a memory of a time when bombs came crashing down and buildings trembled and people perished. Somewhere in me there were the remnants of a feeling, of a terror, that I couldn't control.

I was standing there, frozen, my blood congealed, when James came out of his room and hurried toward me. When I saw him I felt relieved, thinking he was coming to reassure me, to comfort me. But to my surprise, I realized as he stretched out his hands to me that he was laughing. He was delighted with this storm! His exhilaration made him more handsome than ever in his formal suit and dark tie.

"Isn't it exciting? Our first electrical storm this year! It's for our celebration! Mother's not ready yet, but let's go on down. . . ."

He touched me, trying to take my hand. Immediately,

he exclaimed, "Good Lord, you're trembling!" He stared at me, then asked, "Roma! Are you *scared*? My God, we used to love this, you and I! What has happened to you?"

He was truly confounded, standing there in the hall, staring at me with frankly questioning eyes. What a beginning for my brave new self!

The thunder was still rolling, and from the top of the stairs I could see streaks of lightning lighting up the downstairs areas where Susan and another girl were hurrying to draw the draperies and fix the storm windows. I had to overcome my fear. And so something in me, of necessity, stiffened, hardened. I forced myself to give a small laugh.

"You must remember," I said at last, "I've had a few bad days. It was just the sudden shock of the noise. It startled me."

"Of course. Forgive me." He was quick to sympathize. "I keep forgetting. You look so damn well and...and gorgeous!"

He looked me up and down, and I became conscious of myself as a woman as I had never been before. Standing there in my elegant long gown, all made up, I felt like someone else—like Roma Starr? Under his admiring gaze, my confidence came flooding back and, finally, outwardly calm, I walked with him on the stairs.

"Let's get a head start on Mother and André. I've ordered some champagne, and we can sing some old songs. I think the thing I missed most when I went off was the duets we used to have. Remember?"

He squeezed my hand and I mumbled, "Of course," and let him lead me. We were halfway down the beautiful circular stairway when another rumble of thunder began and then rose to a climax that shook the house like a monstrous bomb going off. I couldn't control my terror. James had been holding my hand, but when the explosion came, he pulled me to him and held me tight as though for protection. In my agitation I did not pull away, but clung to him. And then he kissed me, full on the mouth, long and passionately. Just for that moment his kiss seemed a shield against the violence of the rain, against the downpour that was threatening to inundate the house.

When he let me go and I opened my eyes, André was standing at the head of the stairs. I couldn't have felt guiltier had I actually been André's wife. Nor could he have looked more threatening. But James, who surely should have felt guilty, began to laugh and to apologize, not too remorsefully.

"Sorry, old boy, but since marrying you, Roma has become scared of thunderstorms. She needed a little protection." Then tauntingly he added, "Before she met you, she loved storms."

André did not smile in return. In fact, as I glimpsed his clenched fist and white knuckles, I feared that he was about to rush James and punch him. Quickly I left James's side and hurried to André.

"Don't let's spoil the evening," I said. "You know James is my stepbrother and we're old friends—old childhood friends." I said it for James's benefit, of course, as though I believed it

André stood there, unmoving, thrillingly handsome in his black tie and dinner jacket, towering above me and staring at me with eyes smoldering with pain and anger. Why? He did not love me, had no claim on me was not married to me. He knew this. So why?

The minutes passed. James had gone down the stairs and turned into one of the rooms. After a second we heard him at the piano. He was playing chords, as wild as the storm.

"André," I said, grasping one of his hands, "André, come on. It doesn't matter—come on!"

He didn't move. He was standing there like a rock. And his hand was cold, clammy in mine.

"Please," I begged, "please don't spoil everything."

I could see him making an effort to calm down. He shook his head a little and then passed his hand over his brow, covering his eyes for a minute. When he dropped his hand and looked at me again, the anger was gone from his eyes but not the pain. When he spoke, his voice was husky, imperious.

"Don't let him do that again!"

I felt myself flushing, this time with anger. He had no right to order me like that! I wasn't his—his ghost! I almost said that to him, but something made me hold my tongue. I think it was the pain in his eyes.

We stood there for another moment, and then he said in quite another voice, "I was just coming to give you Aunt Clara's present." And he took the small box, prettily wrapped, out of his pocket.

"Thank you," I said formally.

He stepped back to look me over. "I see you've changed your dress. You were right, of course. You look marvelous—a true beauty."

I was flattered and pleased. But then he spoiled it by adding, "But for God's sake, take those earrings off and let your hair down!"

At the words rebellion shot through me. I suppose it was the dictatorial way he said it, but suddenly I was hot all over and angry again. I was *not* going to be pushed around over such little things.

"Don't tell me what to do!" I flared.

And he flared back, "Take them off, I tell you!" And he reached out and snatched at one of them. As he did, of course, I pulled back. The earring fell to the floor

He was quicker than I and immediately stooped and picked it up, rising just as the door of Aunt Clara's room opened.

We froze as she took the few steps toward us. Then André became an instant gentleman and handed me back my earring. He spoke to her while I clipped it back on my ear.

"Good evening, Clara," he said formally. "You look beautiful."

For once I was glad to see her. She had emerged like a living flame in a gown of scarlet chiffon. I immediately turned from André to face her.

"Aunt Clara," I cried, "happy birthday!" And I handed her the box.

"Oh," she said in that high voice, "thank you, my dear. It was very sweet of you to remember."

I had to admire her. She looked what could only be called majestic. She was very thin and tall and, yes, bony, but she had an elegance of carriage, a certain lift of the chin that I knew I would do well to emulate. Her dress was right for her, too. The softness of the flowing chiffon with a low, loosely draped scarf at the neck, which trailed off down her back, did much to mitigate her boniness.

Her poise was unshakable. Thunder, lightning, André's presence—even, I felt, an earthquake—would find her in possession of herself.

Ordinarily, this would have intimidated me, but tonight I was in a mood to fight it. I lifted *my* chin and suggested that we all go down to dinner. André had stood by, silent. He dropped behind us now as we descended the long stairway.

No one tried to speak, for beneath the continuous wild rain and the intermittent thunder we could hear the sound of the piano. James was playing, it seemed, to match the weather. He played very well: the masterful theme of Beethoven's Fifth—the notes of destiny. How clearly I remembered Dr. Peters' explanation, at one of our concerts, of the underlying meaning of the symphony. But even without the explanation I knew, I could feel, the power of those notes. They shook me now with a premonition of *my* destiny, *my* fate.

We continued to the bottom of the stairs, and André, still silent, passed us and led the way in the direction of the music. As we entered the room, it was difficult for me to act as though it were not new to me. I had to control my impulse to exclaim. It was, I suppose, what they call the drawing room, or maybe, in Maine, the music room. But its size and beauty enveloped me and lifted my spirits.

It was decorated completely in gold and white, through the inspiration of Roma herself, I imagined. The room had none of the antique dark mahogany pieces that the other rooms, such as Benjamin's and the library had, but was all glitter and light. The lush carpet was a very pale gold. The draperies, now closed, were the same soft tone so that one felt surrounded by shimmering gold. The furniture was antique white, all of it, even the grand piano. And over all this elegance sparkled a crystal chandelier. It made me giddy, as though neither it nor I were real. When André put a forgiving arm around my waist, I was grateful; it steadied me.

Luckily, James stopped playing his powerful music at once and, giving a quick glance over his shoulder, began "Happy Brithday to You." It seemed to lighten everybody's mood, and as we walked toward the piano, André and James and I began to sing to Aunt Clara. She beamed with delight and seemed to look ten years younger. Actually, she must have been nearing fifty, but her face was very smooth, her skin pulled tight over a fine bone structure, her eyes very much alive, bright, but hard. Her eyes were the one thing that could make me believe what André had said of her—that she was, indeed, a scheming devil. But I brushed that aside, preferring for tonight to try to be friendly with everyone.

When we finished our little tribute to Clara, James jumped from the piano and kissed his mother, then proceeded to act as host. In a corner he had had set up a little table with crystal glasses and champagne on ice. Before we knew it, he was over there, preparing things. It occurred to me as we gathered around that André, not James, should be taking charge of the drinks. And yet André seemed not to care or even to concern himself with the proceedings. He stood next to me brooding as ever.

Suddenly the cork popped, sending a stream of foam into the air. James poured quickly, and we drank a toast to Clara amid another burst of thunder. In my excitement I drank my champagne, which I had never tasted before, in almost one gulp. The fury going on outside seemed to heighten my sensibilities, as though they were competing with the elements. James refilled my glass at once, even as I felt an uneasy movement from André close by my side. Annoyed, I moved away over to the piano and picked up Clara's gaily wrapped gift, which she had placed there upon entering.

"Aunt Clara," I said warmly, "why don't you open your birthday gift?"

Clara was sipping her champagne slowly, daintily, as she followed me to the piano. She did not, however, accept her gift but instead scrutinized me. Carefully, critically, she looked me up and down. Finally she announced, "You look marvelous, my dear." Then she stepped close and stared fixedly at the side of my face.

"I see you are wearing earrings—though you vowed you never would, never could."

She actually touched my face with her icy fingers and lightly turned it to examine, so I thought, the earrings. But it was not the earrings she was interested in.

"You really must tell me—I've been so curious—however did you get rid of that ugly little birthmark?"

The question struck me like a physical blow. I leaned against the piano for support. In a painful flash I remembered the small, raised, dark red mark close to Roma's ear that I had seen that last night in the hospital. Of course she would never have worn anything to make it conspicuous. Too late I realized what André had been trying to save me from.

But he was speaking now with his arm suddenly, affectionately, around my shoulders. "Those doctors in Paris are really fabulous. They can do anything. It's quite a good job, don't you think?"

"Good?" she exclaimed. "Incredible, I'd say!" And she quite unashamedly ran her finger over the spot where Roma's birthmark would have been. "Not even a scar! And you know how I took you to doctors in New York—the very best plastic surgeons. They all said it was impossible, quite useless to try; it was too deep. They said—I remember it distinctly—you should brush your hair over it and forget it. But you were such a perfectionist that you wept. You wanted to wear earrings. And now...."

Here, providentially, the crashing thunder broke out again. The heavens seemed to open up in a wild fury, shaking the house, rattling the storm blinds, and sending out furious bolts of lightning. The noise was deafening. Even Clara's clarion voice could not be heard. Then, as we all stood startled into silence, through the open door came Satan like a bolt of lightning himself.

He ran crazily around the room, over chairs and sofas, leaping into the air, onto the piano, running across the keys, and then up the curtains, all the way to the ceiling. There was no stopping him. We just stood gaping until he voluntarily came down. He paused for a moment in the center of the room, arched his back, and hissed and spat at all of us as though we were responsible for the fury outside. Then he tore out the door.

André sprang to life and ran after him, shouting, "Who the devil let him out? He goes crazy when there's a storm!"

James, too, came to life and swore, "That damn wildcat! He ought to be done away with!" He glared at me, and his face became masklike, as I had seen it on the rocks.

I shivered, still silent, still stunned, when Clara came down on me too. "I told you yesterday that cat must go. Can't you see he's become dangerous? Must we all be terrorized?"

I was grateful when André came back into the room. He was flushed and a little breathless, but at least he had a sense of humor. He laughed as he explained, "That little scamp! We can't find him anywhere. I suppose he's hiding under something. Susan's fairly new here. She didn't have time to learn that we have to lock him up when there's a storm coming."

"I don't remember your having to lock him up, Roma. I remember you carrying him around on your shoulder. You could always control him. But now—"

"He's grown old, Clara, since you were last here. He's not a kitten anymore," André was quick to explain. "And you know storms always excite animals. Anyhow, he's done no harm—except to the draperies."

He laughed then picked up the open champagne bottle and refilled our glasses. "Come, let's toast Aunt Clara once more and then go in. Everything's ready."

I could sense his heightened tension. I knew he didn't want to leave time to return to the subject of my birthmark. And, heaven knows, neither did I. Again I swallowed my drink quickly, although I could feel myself becoming a little lightheaded. Then André graciously offered his arm to Clara, and James delightedly led me toward the dining room.

Susan had done a magnificent job. The table couldn't have been more elegant, with its white damask cloth and gold-banded china and crystal glasses. The centerpiece—a large, shallow, green-tinted pool of water with white flowers floating in it—was a triumph. The strong fragrance of gardenias floated up into the air. The candles burning in the two tall, three-pronged silver candlesticks were reflected in the water and sent shimmering ripples through it. The placid idyllic setting, which contrasted so sharply with the wildness of the night, brought momentary peace to me. Please, God, I prayed silently, let everything go smoothly.

James, standing in back of my chair, pulled it out for me with a chivalrous flourish. And there, curled up in a ball, hidden up to that moment by the tablecloth, was Satan. It didn't take him even a second to be on his feet, his hair and short tail standing up straight, his gleaming, fluorescent eyes wide and flashing from one to the other of us. There was a tense moment before James gave the chair an impatient shake and shouted, "Scat."

But Satan was not to be intimidated. He merely dug his claws into the padded chair seat and spat at James, following that with a low threatening growl.

Clara moved protectively toward James. "Be careful," she ordered, "he'll spring at you!" Then turning to me, she demanded, "*Do* something! Or are you going to let him eat at the table with us?"

I heard the terror in her voice and saw the situation as in a still photograph: four frightened people held at bay around a table by a bobcat who was glaring at us. In my slightly inebriated state it struck me as humorous and, offguard, I gestured lovingly toward the animal. At my incautious movement, André dashed to my side.

"Don't!" he shouted as he pulled my arm back, causing me to lose my balance. I fell against the table, shaking it just as Satan sprang at me, landing on my shoulder. Immediately, I felt the pain from his claws and screamed.

André, acting on reflex, gave Satan a swift push. This caused the cat to produce a stream of scratches down my arm and it threw him right onto the table. Then there was havoc!

Satan splashed into the pool of water and proceeded to knock over the lit candles. Before we knew it, he had jumped off the table, dragging with him the cloth, which had caught in his claws. Glasses and dishes clattered to the floor as the tablecloth burst into flame.

It was pandemonium: Clara screaming, James and André tearing off their jackets to smother the fire, Susan and Harry running in from the kitchen with pails of water, and me trying to help by stamping on the flames on the floor.

One of the last things I remember of that nightmare was Clara running from the room, her flowing scarf on fire. I yanked at it, pulled it off, and stamped on it, feeling the heat scorch my sandals. Then suddenly, my own gown caught fire at the hem. I screamed, terrified, and immediately someone threw a bucket of water at me, drenching me. I gasped. Between the water and the smoke, I was almost unable to breathe.

André gave me a push, yelling, "Get out, we'll manage!"

Someone—I think it was Harry—called out that the fire department was coming. The flames seemed to be consuming the room. The rug was smoldering, and some sparks had caught the draperies, but André called out again, "It's all right, we've got it under control. Roma—go!"

I turned and ran into Emma, who saw my scratches and cried, "You're bleeding! Get out of here! Come!"

As she dragged me out, I heard the fire engines approaching. I suddenly realized the house might burn down. Then I caught Emma's arm.

"Grandfather!" I cried. "We've got to get him out!"

CHAPTER SIXTEEN

BUT THE HOUSE DID NOT BURN DOWN. And Grandfather
Benjamin, well sedated, slept peacefully through all the
turmoil. André had been right; everything had been
under control by the time the firemen arrived. And long
before midnight we were in our separate rooms, ready
to forget the disastrous party. Emma bathed and
dressed my scratches and gave me a tranquilizer. And so
I slept.

Nevertheless, on the following morning I awoke with
a sense of foreboding. At first I thought it was because
of the overcast sky and my first sight of the Maine fog.
There appeared to be a film over the world; when I rose
and went to the window to look at the ocean, it wasn't
there. Everything seemed to have disappeared.

All that was left was the mournful sound of the
breakers, echoed by the buoys and pierced in a muffled
way by the mewling gulls. And through it all, hanging
heavy in the air, was a feeling of impending doom.

The house had not burned down, but something in
me, it seemed, had burned out.

When Emma brought up my breakfast, she tried to be
cheerful. She talked more than usual, giving me all the
news of the house. Apparently, there had been a great
deal of damage but only to the dining room, and everything could be restored. André had left early for Boston; he had said he'd be back toward evening. And
Clara was staying in bed, shattered by last night's ex-

perience. A bundle of old newspapers had arrived for her, so she would be well occupied. James had inquired about me and wanted to come in to see me, but Emma had advised him to wait until later, so he was sitting with Benjamin now. She had warned him not to upset Benjamin by telling him of last night's excitement.

When I questioned her about Satan, she threw up her hands. "That animal! All the damage he's caused! And he's given you some terrible scratches. Aren't you afraid of him?"

"Of course not," I lied, remembering how Roma had loved him. "He was just on edge from the storm, like everyone else."

"But he could have burned the house down!"

"That was because James pushed the chair and spooked him. That's what started everything." I had to defend him, for Roma's sake.

"Well, you be careful. He *is* a wild beast."

"Have you seen him this morning?" I asked.

"No. But when I do, I'll give him a wide berth."

She left me alone then. For a while I sat idle, just staring. I didn't have much appetite. I nibbled on a piece of toast and had a few bites of scrambled egg. Even the coffee couldn't revitalize me. I finally pushed it away and wandered about the room. I had no impetus to dress, to do anything. Perhaps it was a reaction from the night before, but a terrible lethargy seemed to be overcoming me. I went to the window and stared out into the fog. It seemed like my life. A wall of nothing. A blind alley.

In an effort to change my mood, I turned away again and paced around the room, almost angrily, using the anger to fight my depression. It was either that or tears—and I was sick of tears. So many tears, so little joy.

I had tried last night, I had really tried. Oh, I was going to play the part of Roma all right! I was going to be strong and happy. And what followed? Disaster. Sheer disaster. I didn't know how to be strong and happy. I didn't know how (why not face it?) to be Roma.

Roma, Roma—what did I know of you, after all? I knew you as a loving and beautiful girl in the last week of your life. I knew you as a woman with a neglectful husband whom I had hated because of that neglect. Later I learned that you had once loved James and probably many others, that you were wild and reckless, perhaps ruthless. Oh, Roma, you and I are very different people. I don't criticize you for what you were, but I am different. I am one of those tortured souls who, like André, will love only once. I feel it in my bones. Maybe that's what we have in common, André and I. Maybe that's why I am so drawn to him.

I stopped pacing right in the middle of the room. I stood very still, my hands clasped over my heart. Yes, I had to face it. Quietly, secretly, I had to face it. *I loved him*. And of course he did not, could not, love me. He could only love his old love, his one love, his ghostly Sybil. He, as well as I, was trapped.

Slowly I walked over and leaned against the chest of drawers, facing the mirror that hung over it. I stared at myself as at a stranger. I had changed in the few days I had been here. Five days. It could have been five years! The change was in my eyes mostly. As I remembered them back at the hospital, they had been clear translucent green, with a little hope showing through. Now they were dark with tumult.

I looked down then to avoid seeing my pain so plainly and noticed the collection of little silver and gold boxes strewn about on top of the dresser. Someone—Roma, or perhaps her mother—had had a penchant for them.

Idly, I fingered one of them, then another, opening them. Some of them, small as they were, were lined in silk or velvet. One even had a minute key in a lock. I twisted it and opened it. And there inside on a red velvet pad was a child's locket.

I suddenly felt that I had invaded Roma's privacy deeper than I had any right to. My hand trembled a little as I lifted the locket out of the box. Yet, I could not stop myself. I had to open it. When I did, I saw two baby faces staring up at me. The faces were too tiny to be recognizable, but I assumed one, perhaps both, were Roma as a child. But it wasn't that that froze me. It was another feeling: the feeling, the *knowledge* that like many children, I too had once had a locket similar to this one. Where was mine now?

Slowly I replaced the locket and closed the box. Unexpectedly the tears started down my cheeks. I went into the dressing room for a tissue, and then I sank down on the bench at the dressing table and wept.

It was in the midst of my tears that I heard a sound close by—a faint meow. I looked up and there was Satan, poking his nose out from a crack in the closet door. I got up and rolled the door back far enough for him to get out. He must have been there all night, having fled from the turmoil downstairs, and got himself locked in. This time we looked at each other more charitably. He was, I thought, a little humbled. And I was too sad to be very frightened. I went out to the bedroom and sat in one of the chairs. He followed, stopping directly in front of me.

As I dried my tears, I spoke to him. "Are you sorry, Satan, for all the trouble you caused? You didn't really mean to do it, did you—cause the fire and give me all these scratches?"

I couldn't bear to think he hated me, not this morning. As I pleaded with him, he watched me curiously, twisting his head to one side. I suppose he caught my sympathetic tone, for he came and rubbed against my legs and gave out a raucous *prump*. I wanted to pat his head, but I had just enough fear left to prevent me. Then I realized that if he'd been here all night he was probably hungry. I got up and went to the tray.

"Come," I said, "come, Satan," and held out a bit of the cold scrambled egg. He came right over and started to eat from my hand. When I sat on the edge of the bed, he jumped up beside me, and I bravely fed him the rest of the egg, feeling the roughness of his warm tongue on my palm. And watching him as he ate, I realized for the first time how it must be for him. Deprived of his natural companions, he was now deprived of the only person in the world whom he had trusted and loved. How lonely he must be, waiting and hoping every day for her return.

"Dear Satan," I tried to tell him as he finished eating and began to wash his paws, "your mistress is not coming home. She has left us all—forever."

He looked up at me then, and though his eyes were as wild and glistening as ever, for just a moment I seemed to recognize a pleading expression in them, as though he were saying, "Love me. I need you, for I am all alone now."

"I will love you, Satan," I whispered, "if you'll let me—for I, too, am all alone." And I stretched out on the bed and buried my head in the pillow.

In my unhappiness, I must have fallen asleep again. It was late afternoon when I awoke. Satan had gone, and I could see the shadows darkening the room. What woke me was a sound by my bed; someone was placing something on the little table next to me. It took me a moment to rouse myself, and by the time I had turned to see a glass of milk sitting on the table, the person who brought it in was leaving. It wasn't Emma, although I couldn't really make out the dark figure just closing the door. It must have been James. I suppose he'd come in with the milk, seen that I was sleeping, and just left it. Good old James. He was still trying!

But I didn't want to see him. I didn't want to see anybody. That heavy feeling of foreboding was still with me, and suddenly, there in the half-light and the quiet of the house, it surfaced. I realized that I was worried about that story of Roma's birthmark. Clara had been frankly disbelieving. Even James had stared strangely. And I hadn't had time to talk to André—not that that would have helped. He would be no comfort now. He would be angry with me for having worn those earrings with my hair pulled back, drawing attention to the very thing that would give me away.

Suddenly I was tired, tired of it all—except for Benjamin. One thought of him, and I rose from the bed. I hadn't been in to see him all day. What would he think? Quickly I smoothed my hair, taking care this time to keep it in front of my ears, and then slipped into a robe. I wanted to see Benjamin, for his sake—and for my own. I always felt better, a little more useful after I had seen him, as though there were some justification for my life.

As I was about to leave, my eye was caught by the glass of milk that had been left for me. I decided to take it down to Benjamin. Perhaps if I urged him he would drink it. Emma was always complaining that he wouldn't eat.

In the waning afternoon light, I hurried down the hall, anxious to enter his room without meeting anyone.

When I opened the door, the room seemed warm— too warm, with a slight odor of medicine, the atmosphere of a sickroom. Emma wasn't there; she must have left him to go downstairs to eat. Glad to be alone with him, I walked quietly over to his bedside and placed the milk on a small table that was pushed up close to his bed. Emma had arranged the furniture that way since Benjamin had gained some use of his arms and insisted, as much as possible, on feeding himself when he did eat.

I looked down at his giant waxen face, at the pale, once-firm lips. There was a drop of perspiration on his forehead, and I took a handkerchief and dabbed at it gently. At the touch his eyelids fluttered and opened. His hand moved shakily across his chest and touched mine.

"Grandfather," I said, sitting beside him, "I've brought you some milk."

He patted my hand gently. "My dear girl," he whispered, "my child."

He seemed weaker than usual. As I reached for the milk, he shook his head.

"Later," he said, "not now."

"Don't you want me to help you?"

He shook his head again, then said, "I can take it myself—later"

I saw that Emma had got him some straws, and I had to admire his independence.

I bent down and pressed my cheek against his hand. I had that feeling again: that great warmth, that unexplainable closeness. It flowed through his ancient, weakened body into my being, and suddenly I had to put my arms around him and hug him: I had to say, "My darling Grandfather Benjamin, I love you."

I said it as I had never spoken to another human being. I said it as though he belonged to me—heartbreakingly, because I wanted it to be true. I felt his hand touch my hair, and then we both were still and silent for a second.

When I looked up, I thought his face looked more peaceful than I had ever seen it. But I caught a tear in the corner of his eye. I brushed it away gently and got up. I thought it would be better for him if I left. I was afraid I was putting him through some emotional trauma. Perhaps he was reliving some moment of his life with Roma. I kissed him, then crossed to the door. As I opened it, Satan ran in past me. I let him by, then I hurried back down the hall and into Roma's room, thankful not to have met anyone.

I stood for a moment against the door, feeling particularly weak, almost suffocated. All at once I had a great longing for fresh air. I went to the French windows, flung them open and stepped out onto the balcony. Ah, that sea air, blowing strongly now, full in my face! The fog had lifted, and there was just the faintest mist as the evening drew on. I could see the sea again. Instantly invigorated, I stood there quietly breathing my life back into me.

I was so lost in the sensations that I became aware of the voices only gradually. They were coming from next door—from Clara's room. I glanced over and saw that its French windows were open. The voices grew louder, the voices of Clara and James. I distinctly heard James say, "But it's not true! It *can't* be true. She's right here in this house."

"You fool!" It was Clara's voice, painfully clear, hissing back at him. "It says right here in the paper that she *died* in the hospital—that her remains were cremated and are being shipped back to the United States."

I heard James groan. "It can't be true! Papers make mistakes."

"Not the London *Times*. And it's in the Boston paper, too."

"But...but..." he stammered.

"You *are* a fool. You don't *want* to believe it. But you told me yourself that first day that she didn't *feel* like Roma."

"But...but..." he continued to stutter in agitation.

"Last night—that was when I was certain. Oh, I had noticed that her birthmark wasn't there—but it could have been cleverly covered. But last night after I examined it and *felt* it, I knew something was wrong."

"Doctors are clever now. They do things—fantastic things."

"No doctor could remove that mark. It was too deep. I went with her myself to the best surgeons. *I'm* not a fool even if you are. That girl is an imposter. She's clever. She knows that Roma is dead and that she looks like her and that her poor old half-blind grandfather won't know. She's posing as Roma to get her fortune."

There was a silence. I stood frozen, holding my breath. I was about to flee when James spoke again in a horrible hoarse voice, as though something was just dawning on him. "By God! I think you're right. Now it all makes sense—the strange way she acted. And that André—I hated him the minute I saw him. They're in it together."

"Of course they are. Don't you see? Roma is dead and they're out to make off with her fortune!"

"We'll call the police! They're *criminals*!"

I ran back into the room and closed the doors. It had happened—I was found out! I stood there terrified, my heart pounding, my knees weakened to the point of buckling. As if drunk, I stumbled across the room. I leaned against the dresser and tried with all my will-power to think. To *think*. What should I do? What *could* I do? Of course. I had to find André, to tell him. He would have to explain—explain that we meant no harm, that we were not criminals. I could hardly stand. For a moment I sank down into the chair, but soon fear, which can strengthen as well as weaken, forced me up.

I had to go up to the studio, to where he kept himself locked in most of the time—to the upper floor. Perhaps he had already come home; pray God he had, for it was getting on toward evening.

Warily I opened the door and, seeing no one, flew like the wind to the door at the end of the hall. Without knocking, I opened it and found a flight of stairs. Waiting for nothing, I started up. When I reached the top, I found myself looking into an enormous room. It was a workroom, a studio with easels and canvases strewn about, books lining one wall, a desk, a single leather chair and a cold fireplace. This room was bare, ascetic. Here lives a solitary man, it said.

But where was the man? He had not come home yet. What was I to do? Wait for him here or go back to Roma's room? Suddenly no place seemed safe. I stood wringing my hands, unable to think for myself. Oh, why wasn't he here? He had got me into this. Why had he left me here alone? I couldn't explain it, but *he* could. He could tell them that we only meant to save Benjamin a shock. He could make them believe it...or could he? They didn't like or trust him, either.

I felt a wave of nausea overcoming me and a kind of whirling in my head. I didn't want to faint up here in this strange room. I struggled to steady myself. I would have to get back to Roma's room and lock myself in until he came.

A note. I would leave him a note and tell him to come to me at once.

I went to the desk for some paper and a pen. I opened

the drawer and picked up a large white pad. And right
beneath it, leaping up before my eyes, was a little black
box strangely like the one in which I had carried my
ring. I stared at it, my feelings suspended. As in a
trance, I removed the lid and there, leering up at me as
in so many of my nightmares, was my ring—my satyr
ring.

I stood staring down at it, so many feelings teeming
through me, I scarcely knew which one was uppermost.
First, I suppose, was elation. I had recovered my one
possession, my one link to my past. I picked up the ring
and slipped it onto my finger. Never, I vowed silently,
never would I take it off again.

But as I sank down into the chair by the desk and
closed my eyes, other emotions began to take hold. A
terrible wariness crept over me—wariness of André.
What was my ring doing in his desk drawer? He had lied
to me. He had told me my flight bag had been left at the
airport, that he hadn't had time to go to pick it up. But
with sudden enlightenment I knew that he had had it
here all the while, that he had been withholding it from
me on purpose. But why?

The answer came almost immediately: to keep me
here, as security. How could he have known that I
would never leave the house without it? But he had. I
knew it instinctively. He had to keep me here to use me.
But for what? How?

With James's words, "They're criminals," ringing in
my ears, a terrible shudder ran through me. Was
André—the André I had come to love—a criminal?
Everything in me rebelled against the idea, but there was
too much mystery about him, too many questions unan-
swered. I had always felt it, that mystery. And now I
knew he had hidden my ring, the key to keeping me
here, to making me a partner in his crime.

I sat at the desk, paralyzed. In a blinding flash I saw myself accused, arrested, convicted. Of what? Not just of stealing a passport and entering a country illegally, but of fraud. Of conspiracy. Of attempting to steal a fortune by impersonating a dead girl.

And then, clutching the ring, I flew down the stairs. I didn't realize I was making decisions; I just moved, without hesitation, without question. At the foot of the stairs, I stopped long enough to see that no one was in the hall. Then I raced to Roma's room.

There I dressed myself in my own clothes. They seemed shabby and thin as I put them on, but it was of little consequence I was Sara Smith, not Roma Starr. I found the thought strangely comforting. I buttoned up my tweed coat carefully, as though it mattered, as though it would protect me. And then I pulled on my little black hat and picked up my old purse.

The tears started to come. but I held them back. Not now, not now; no time for tears. I took one last look around the room, one backward glance, and seemed to say goodbye to Roma all over again. I dared not think of Benjamin. I dared not think of Satan. And above all, I dared not think of André.

As I cautiously opened the door, I heard voices, muffled now, still in conflict, coming from Clara's room. Quickly, before I should meet anyone, I hastened down the stairs and out the front door, closing it behind me ever so quietly, ever so sadly.

As the evening shadows began to thicken, I walked out the curving driveway and onto the road. The road to... where?

I turned to my right because that was the way I had seen André drive off. That had to be the way to town. As I walked, the sound of the sea followed me. The wonderful. terrible sound of the sea. I stopped a little way up the road and stood leaning against a pine tree.

I wanted to take one last look at the sea, rolling with life and terror and mystery. And a last look, too, at the Starr Mansion, where, for a few days, I had had a home and a grandfather. Where I had loved an old man and where I had, for a little while, and foolishly, loved a young man.

Then, standing there, the tears finally came. Helplessly, I let them. It didn't matter. Nothing mattered. I walked on toward the town

CHAPTER SEVENTEEN

THEY SAY there is some special strength in the air on the coast of Maine. Iron, perhaps. And I guess it is true, for I started out on that unfamiliar road, between towering pines and rising cliffs on my left and the ocean surging wildly on my right, like a lost child being buffeted against the rocks. But by the time I had reached the town—a quaint summer resort, all quiet and closed up now—I had changed to the rock itself.

Something had happened along the way. I had become myself again. Having lost everything at the Starr Mansion, I now had regained my own individuality. Sara Smith might not remember her past life, but she stood for something. She was real.

After all, I told myself as I hurried along into the stinging wind, the whole thing was a mirage, a fantastic imagining. It wasn't *you* who was there. It was a shadow, a dream—like all your other dreams. And then and there I made myself remember the girl who had had the courage to take a chance, the girl who had left the Ellis Hospital in London to make a life of her own. Well, here she was again. She had just been set back five days by a ruthless man. I shuddered at the thought of André and the thought that I had loved him. But this time I remained hard. I was going to look out for myself, to take up where I had left off the day I walked out of the hospital.

And so, almost without realizing it, I arrived at a

small bus terminal just before dark. The sign leaped
up at me and forced me to stop. I took a deep breath
and tried to straighten my hat and look like any normal traveler. I didn't want to be noticed. I walked up to
the ticket window and slipped one of Roma's $20 bills
toward an impassive, tight-lipped man. He gave me a
sharp glance as I said, "Boston, please."

Then, as he counted out my change and gave me my
ticket, he said with a Yankee twang, "You're lucky.
Last bus. Right over there."

Thankfully, I boarded the half-empty bus. It started
up almost immediately. During the ride—how long, I
have no idea—I closed my eyes, determined to suspend
my thoughts, my feelings. But it couldn't be done. I
knew I would have to go somewhere at the end of the
line. But where? Suddenly I sat up sharply. Of course I
couldn't stay in Boston. André would know too many
people, too many places. And Clara would too. I would
have to take another bus, or train, or plane. But to
where?

My question was answered when we arrived at North
Station and I heard, close by, the shriek of a train
whistle. I would go on to New York! The very thought
raised my spirits. New York, the great metropolis. No
one would ever find me there. There I would be free to
start my life, my real life, the one I would shape for
myself.

By following signs, I found my way to the railroad
terminal and there I bought my ticket to New York. I
was told the train would not leave till nine o'clock. That
gave me two hours. I would use the time to eat a good
meal. I went into a restaurant right in the station, where
I could keep my eye on the clock, and I ate like a man.
As I paid the waiter, I silently blessed Roma for having
left so much money (there were still five twenties) in her

case. I knew I would have got nowhere with my English pounds.

By the time I boarded the train I was feeling fine. I was getting my second wind. A kind of euphoria swept over me. It was a sense of freedom, I suppose, for having left all the pretense behind. But I hadn't reckoned on the long ride to New York. As the monotonous hours passed, I grew weary. My spirits began to flag. I needed sleep and yet I couldn't sleep, as so many of the passengers seemed to be able to do. I looked around enviously at the dozing faces. These people knew where they were headed. All of them were going to homes where they had families, or to hotels with which they were familiar, while I...I stopped myself in midsentence and peered down at my satyr ring.

"Well," I said to that tantalizing face, "this was all your idea. You had better take care of me. You are my only friend."

Then I folded my hand over the ring and began rubbing it as though it were a genie.

I was still rubbing my ring when we plunged into a long black tunnel. Suddenly alert, I sat up. The atmosphere in the train seemed to change. People began talking and reaching for their luggage. Then came the drawn-out announcement of the conductor: "Neeew Yooork City...Graaand Central...."

At his words, my heart started to pound again. I had no luggage, so there was nothing for me to do but sit and wait, but it was difficult. I wanted to move too. I rose once, but the movement of the train promptly shook me back into my seat.

When the train finally stopped, I rose with everyone else and was virtually pushed up the aisle and out the door. I was carried along with the other passengers—up one ramp to the upper landing, down a slanting ramp, and out into an incredible marble station swarming with people. Everyone was rushing and for no reason I rushed, too, joining the confusion, past people, stairs, exits, entrances—until I finally smelled fresh air and saw the street.

There were so many people, all crowding against me. It was difficult to believe that all this excitement was going on in the middle of the night, at two A.M.! There seemed to be nothing but lights and towering buildings and pavement and taxis—taxis everywhere. When one came up and stopped in front of me, I got in just because it was there. It rattled off, bounding a few yards, squeaking to a halt again at the intersection.

"Where to, lady?" the driver shouted at me over his shoulder.

Where to? Where to? I clutched the cold, broken leather seat in the back and answered, "A hotel, please."

"*A* hotel?" he hollered as he swung around in his seat and glared at me. "*What* hotel?"

He was rather frightening, with a cap pulled down over his brow and a big dark mustache. He looked me over with little darting eyes. Then he asked "Whatsa matter? Dontcha know where ya wanna go?"

The street lights changed from red to green, and the cab lurched forward again, zigzagging through a sea of people, around endless other taxis. Brakes squeaked, horns blared. Then we stopped again. This time he pulled up to the curb. We were on a side street.

He turned around to face me again, and I made an effort to direct him.

"I'm sorry," I said with some dignity, "but I'm new here. I'd like a nice hotel. Can you recommend one?"

He laughed a kind of guffaw. "Christ, lady! This

town is full of hotels. It's just a matter of how much you wanna pay.''

"Not...too expensive," I said and added, "but nice.''

After a long searching look, he asked, "How about the YWCA?''

At first I almost leapt at the idea. It sounded safe and wouldn't be too expensive. But just in time it occurred to me that it would be the first place they would look if they should try to find me.

"No," I said firmly, "I don't want the Y.''

"Well, if you wanna go a little way uptown, I know just the place. Near the university. They have residence clubs. Like hotels, but cheaper. Lots of students up there. College kids.''

"That sounds fine. Anything. But let's get out of here.''

"Okay," he said, and we started out again with a violent lunge. I had to hang on to the seat all the way. He talked incessantly—about how there were too many crowds, too many taxis, no room in the city, etcetera. He only added to my confusion. But finally the crowds and the noise seemed to lessen and with an incredible jolt we came to a full stop in front of a place marked Columbia Residence Club.

"Here you are, kid. Home, sweet home.''

He made no move to let me out, so I struggled with the door myself. When I couldn't get it closed, he yelled, "Ya gotta *slam* it, lady.''

So I did. Then I handed him a $20 bill and told him to take what he needed plus a tip. He eyed me fixedly for a second, shrugged and counted out the money, handing me some change. As the cab rattled off, he touched his hand to his cap and yelled back, "Lotsa luck, lady! There's a vacancy sign.''

I stood for a moment before going inside. It was a clear night and the stars were bright, sparkling up there between the tall buildings that lined both sides of the street.

"Lotsa luck, lady." It rang in my ears as I opened the door.

WHEN I AWOKE late the next day, I had a dim memory of having walked into a dark lobby, signed a register, paid out some money and then ridden up in a creaking elevator.

And here I was, still fully clothed, lying on a hard bed with a blanket pulled over me. I was stiff, aching now in every bone of my body. I opened my eyes and looked around the room. It was ugly. Everything was decorated in plaid—the one chair, the rug, the cover on the small table. There was a maple dresser and an old-fashioned lamp. The place was so small, I was sure I could sit on the bed and put my feet on the dresser

Well, what did it matter? I had escaped. I had had to run like a criminal, but here I was safe. I sighed a long deliberate sigh. Of course I was not a criminal, no matter what Clara and James believed. But I was a fool. Yes, a fool, to allow André to bully me into...everything. Here a sharp pain in my heart forced me to sit up. A shudder of shame went through my whole body.

How could I have believed everything he said, followed his every direction like a puppet and then fallen in love with him?

I buried my head in my hands and had to acknowledge the worst shame of all: I still loved him.

But after a minute I shook myself back to reality. He was wicked, I told myself. He trapped me and then hid my ring. He was using me. I would have to forget him. I had to think of nothing and no one but Sara

Smith. Because Sara Smith had things to do—a life to start over.

And so, with a kind of ruthless discipline, for the next two days I made myself do the things I would have done had I not been spirited away to the Starr Mansion.

I managed on the first day to familiarize myself with a little corner of that big city. I took a walk, found a place to eat, passed many shops and bought, in one of them, a pair of pajamas and an inexpensive robe. But, most important, I walked into a large bank and exchanged my English pounds for dollars. I now had enough money to buy another dress. By the end of the day, I felt I had accomplished quite a bit.

But there was one more essential thing I had to do before I could think of anything else, before I could face the enormous task of finding myself a job and starting over. I had to have my hair dyed back to its natural color.

That is how I spent my second day in New York City. It was already growing dark when I returned to my little room at the residence club. A significant change had taken place in me. I had entered the beauty salon a replica of Roma Starr, and I had left it as myself, Sara Smith. Sara Smith with the dark mahogany hair curling about her temples and falling smoothly to her shoulders.

I felt different inside. It was as though Roma's spirit had at last left me free to be myself. As I hurried back to my new home, I whispered, "Goodbye, Roma. Goodbye."

For the first time since leaving the hospital I felt whole again. There was a certain strength in it. For though I had no memory of things past, the present and the future were all mine. It was up to me to make something of them.

And so, back in my little room at last, I lit the shabby lamp and sat down at the table. The first thing I did was to take Roma's leather case from my purse and draw out her passport. I looked at her photo—at her vibrant face and shining eyes—and then, wincing, tore it up. It was something I had to do in order to be free of her. It seemed to be the end of something—the final act of the sad drama I had played for five days.

I touched my ring and looked down at the satyr's face, which had started it all, and asked it, *what next?*

Just then there was a knock at the door.

CHAPTER EIGHTEEN

I SAT STILL, startled. No one knew I was here, and I knew no one in New York. Who could be knocking? It came again. Loud, demanding.

I rose and walked the few steps to the door and opened it. In the half-light stood a powerful man, peering down at me, looking from me to what I guessed was a description of me on a scrap of paper in his hand.

"Are you the girl who registered as Sara Smith?"

I stiffened. Why should I answer him? While I hesitated, he put his foot on the threshold and asked, "May I come in?"

I stood firm, not yielding. "Who are you? What do you want?"

He took a billfold from his pocket and showed me his identification. "I'm Bill Barnes, private investigator. André Tate asked me to find you and bring you back to Maine."

A combination of fury and fear swept through me. What right did André have to drag me back? Did he expect me to face Clara and James and deny what they already knew?

"I'm sorry," I said with all the firmness I could muster. "I'm not going back. You can't make me."

"Of course not. But Mr. Tate thought you would want to come back of your own accord. He sent me to urge you...."

Of my own accord? What did he mean? Had Clara already managed to call the police? Would they be looking for me? But this man was not the police. I would still have time to run.

"I'm not going back with you. Tell Mr. Tate—"

"Please," he said, as he pushed a little way into the room, "let me come in. I must tell you, something has happened. . . ."

It was the way he said, "Something has happened," that sent a chill through me. I let him come in and closed the door after him.

"What. . . has happened?"

"Benjamin Starr is dead."

It struck me like a hammer blow. All this time, I had tried not to think of Benjamin. I didn't want to feel guilty for having left him. And now he was dead.

When I tried to speak, my throat was dry. "What. . . how? Did he have another stroke?"

"I guess so. I really don't know. Mr. Tate didn't explain. He just called me and asked me to try to find you and urge you to come back. He said to tell you to trust him to straighten everything out."

I sat down on the edge of the bed. Trust him! His old refrain! It was because I *couldn't* trust him that I had run away. But now an awful ache was filling me, a guilt that suspended my fear of Clara and the police; guilt for having left Benjamin. Hadn't André warned me that if I left, it would kill him?

Suddenly the fact that I had entered the country with Roma's passport didn't seem to matter. Even the fact that Clara and James knew what André and I had tried to do didn't seem important. If they did call the police, I knew that I ought to be there to defend myself, if nothing else. I should not have run away. Whether I could trust André or not—that was another matter. I would have to go back.

I stood up. "You don't have to come with me," I said, "I can take the train myself."

"I know that, but my instructions were to take good care of you, so we're flying back."

I went to get my coat. Just then Mr. Barnes said, "I see you've colored your hair. I was told you were blond."

Our eyes met. He obviously thought I was trying to disguise myself, whereas it was the other way around—I was trying to become myself. I didn't bother to explain but put on my coat.

Just before I turned to leave with him, the torn scraps of Roma's passport, still on the table, caught my eye. I went over and picked them up and dropped them in the wastebasket.

Goodbye Roma. Goodbye pretense. Whatever I had to face now, I would face as Sara Smith—until, of course, my ring gave up its secret.

"All right," I said, "I'm ready."

AND SO WE WENT to La Guardia Airport and took the plane back to Boston. Mr. Barnes and I had little to say to each other, although he tried to make conversation. He told me how he had found me: a day spent checking the cabbies at Grand Central Station. He was rather pleased with himself, I thought.

As for me, it didn't matter anymore. Everything was different. Grandfather Benjamin was dead. I felt an emptiness that could not have been worse had I known him my whole life. In a way, the few days that I had been with him in his house now seemed like my whole life. It was, surely, the best of the little life I could remember. I had had someone to love, someone who loved me.

But I had run away—in fear for myself, without

thinking of him. Had he awakened and called for me? And had they told him I was a fraud—that I was not his granddaughter at all, but some stranger trying to fool him?

Oh, God! Of course he would have had another stroke!

By the time we landed in Boston, I was silent and lost in my thoughts. After phoning the house, Mr. Barnes hired a car, and he drove us out of the city and on up to the coast of Maine.

I rolled the window down and let the fresh cold wind blow full in my face. It sent waves of emotion coursing through me. It was almost as though I were returning home after a long absence.

And yet I shivered a little. I began to think about reentering the Starr Mansion as myself, Sara Smith. How would I face André? And Clara and James? I didn't know. All I knew was that the scene would be different from before, because my concern was not for myself anymore. My reason for returning was not to justify myself or to excuse myself to any of them. My reason was to be with Benjamin—now, too late. I wanted to be with him for Roma's sake and for my own. I wanted to stand by him once more and speak to his stilled heart and confess. Perhaps no one would understand that—not even André.

Oh André, André— My thoughts stopped, frozen. automatically my hand reached out, feeling for my ring. I remembered the way he had tricked me into staying by hiding it from me. And when I had run to him for help and found my ring in his drawer, all my illusions about him had crumbled.

The car came to an abrupt stop; I looked up and saw that we had arrived. There it was, all dark now and fore-boding, the stately old house from which I had fled in fear. The house in which Benjamin lay dead—because I had gone.

As Mr. Barnes got out of the car and ran around to open my door, a light appeared in the front hall, and as I stepped from the car, the front door opened. I tried not to look to see who it was, but the headlights were still on, flooding the front steps, and in the artificial light I saw him, a tall pale figure in a deep red robe, rushing toward me. I barely had time to turn away when he had his arms around me, turning me back around.

"You're here," André was saying, "thank God, you're here!"

It wasn't the way I had planned to meet him. It was difficult for me to hold my own, but I stiffened, holding myself aloof. This time I would have things my way.

"Yes," I said coldly, "I'm here. Can we go inside?"

Mercifully, at that instant Mr. Barnes turned off the lights and called out, "We made it as fast as we could."

He joined us then, and in some confusion we all went into the house.

It was dark and deathly quiet inside. Everyone had gone to bed, of course. It must have been past midnight. The house felt different to me—empty, the heart gone out of it.

Mr. Barnes was saying, "I've got to get right back to town. I can't wait, really. There's some important—"

Then André interrupted, "But you can't go right away. Susan left some sandwiches and something for us to drink."

The library door was open, and I could see a blazing fire in the old flagstone fireplace. A coffee table was set with food and cups and saucers. André was holding onto my arm.

"Come in," he said, "both of you. Relax and have something...."

But I pulled back. I was not going to relax with the two of them as though I were a lost child being returned to the family bosom. I was a stranger here who had been tricked by this man and used for some purpose. What I had to say could not be said over coffee and sandwiches.

"I'm sorry," I said, carefully disengaging my arm from his, "I don't want anything. Good night, Mr. Barnes. Thank you for helping me."

And I turned and started up the stairs. I could feel André standing there a little stunned. After I had gone a few steps, he called, "I'll be right with you, dear."

I continued up, my hand trembling a little on the banister. I was not as calm as I had intended to be. The house itself was doing something to me. I remembered, nostalgically, the little nick in the banister halfway up, the carpet where an occasional footprint showed. And the smell, the overall smell of—what was it? Pine? Cedar? It gave me a sense of "home," of returning to familiar blessed ground. It almost frightened me, for it was important for me not to become attached to anything here. This was a goodbye visit to Benjamin; it was not a homecoming.

At the top of the stairs I stopped and looked down the hall, my heart thudding against my ribs. Benjamin... grandfather. I felt something pulling me toward his room. Was he in there, silent and cold as the rocks of the sea?

Did he feel me coming to him? Would he understand and forgive? Silently, swiftly, I walked up to his door. My hand quietly turned the knob and I stepped in.

There was a small light on over the bed. But the bed was empty. Too late; I had come too late. Everything in the room was in perfect order; no medicine bottles, no empty glasses or extra linens. The dim light threw shadows around the room. The great dark leather chair that I had never seen him use seemed pitifully empty. The secretary-desk with its top-heavy books, its pen and inkwell, seemed waiting for his hand to touch them. And the little table where I had placed the glass of milk that last night was cleared now. Empty. Only the smell of the sickroom lingered on; only the feel of his presence hovered there. And everything seemed to be waiting, waiting.

Softly I closed the door, then went over to kneel by his bed. I knelt there for a long time, silently talking to him. I told him all the things I couldn't say before. I told him how it was with me—how I didn't know who I was, and how I had met Roma and had come, not to take her place, but to comfort him, to keep my promise to her. I asked him to forgive me for coming—and for going. I dropped my head down over my hands and said a kind of prayer, weeping quietly.

I don't know how long I remained there; I didn't hear the door open. I didn't hear his step behind me. But suddenly I felt his hands on my shoulders.

I twisted around and looked at André, his face drawn and white, his eyes dark and questioning. "For God's sake, why did you do it? Why did you run away?"

I stood up, the tears I had been shedding for Benjamin suddenly frozen on my face.

"It's your fault!" I accused him. "You made me do it and you made me kill him."

"You don't know what you're saying!"

"Oh, but I do! I didn't come here meaning to deceive him. And I wouldn't have gone away if I could really have trusted you!"

"But you're wrong—you *can* trust me! You're mistaken—"

"Am I? Am I mistaken—" I thrust my hand in front of him "—about *this*?"

He drew back, staring at my ring as though I had slapped him. Before he could catch his breath, I went on, "Yes. It's my ring, my *lost* ring. I found it in your desk drawer. You didn't think I'd ever go looking for it there, did you? Well, I *wasn't* looking for it. I was looking for *you*. I ran upstairs, away from Clara and James, because I needed you. With you there, nothing else would have mattered. Clara could have told them everything. She could have told them I wasn't Roma, that I was only pretending to be. She could have called her lawyer, she could even have called the police—"

"I wouldn't have let her. I would have protected you—"

"That's what I thought, too. I ran to find you and you weren't there. You were never there when I needed you! You left me alone here, to cope and to conceal—"

"I was only trying to get some help. I had to go to Boston to see a doctor. You could have—"

"Oh, yes, I know. I could have *trusted* you! But why should I trust you when you took my ring and hid it from me all the while? Why should I trust you when you didn't trust *me*? I did what you wanted. I played your game. I followed your plans and deceived everybody, made a fraud of myself, for *you*. For something you were trying to pull off.

"What was it? What had you planned that you couldn't tell me, that you couldn't trust me with? Why did you think you had to keep me a prisoner? Oh yes, you knew my ring was important to me. You knew I wouldn't go away without it, so you took it and hid it. You had a reason for keeping me here that you didn't want to tell me about, didn't you? *Didn't you?* You wanted me here at all costs. Why?"

My voice had risen to a shrill pitch and I was facing

him with my fists clenched. Suddenly he grabbed my wrists and, holding them tight, forced me down on the edge of the bed, towering over me.

"Be quiet! Be quiet and listen to me!" He glared down at me, fire in his eyes. "Yes, yes." His voice was hoarse and horrible. "I wanted you here at all costs, I admit it. And yes, I had a reason of my own. All I asked of you was a little faith! But I see it was too much to ask. Forgive me. But I thought—I thought...." He hesitated, overcome by emotion.

I saw the pupils of his eyes flicker and grow dark; his lips gave a little twitch. It was plain he didn't know how to go on. For an interminable second we remained rigid—I, glaring up at him, and he, leaning over me, still gripping my wrists. Then he did a strange thing. He suddenly loosened his grip and bent his head down and kissed my ring.

For a moment I waited unsteadily—shocked, holding back. Then, all at once, I gave in and leaned over and pressed my cheek against his soft, thick hair. He sank down on the bed beside me. And it was all over. All my resentment, all my suspicions, were washed away.

Feeling him close, feeling him there beside me, I absolved him. He couldn't be guilty of anything wrong.

He looked up at last, his agate eyes moist. I seemed to see inside them this time, to the dark mysterious person hidden in there. I seemed to know him as I had never known him before. Of course I should have trusted him. I wanted to love him. I knew he needed me.

I opened my arms to him, and he folded his around me. And so we remained, soothing one another, drawing life from one another until the intensity of his body, the touch of his lips against mine, sent a thrill of surrender through me.

In that moment I felt as though I had recovered my

life, found a missing part of my soul. I didn't think I would ever deny it again. No matter about my ring. No matter his secrets, his unexplained plans. No matter if the ghost of Sybil remained forever between us. I was home when I was in his arms.

CHAPTER NINETEEN

IT WAS A LONG WHILE before either of us spoke. What was there to say? I had come to ask Benjamin to forgive me and had stayed to love the man I had hated. Would Benjamin mind?

While I was wondering about it and feeling Benjamin's presence in every shadow of the room, André began to twist a strand of my hair in his fingers. It was then I realized he must have been surprised to see me with dark hair in place of Roma's shining gold. Before I could say anything, he whispered, as though it were a secret between us, "I like what you've done to your hair."

I decided then to tell him it was my own color.

"I didn't dye it to try to disguise myself, you know. It's really—"

"It's really your own color." He supplied the sentence for me.

I turned to face him. "How did you know?"

He smiled half-secretively, half-triumphantly. "Don't be angry. I have to tell you. I know. I know...all about you."

I sat up. He sat up, too, and touched my hand.

"Right after I brought you here, I had to call Ellis Hospital about Roma. And I talked to Dr. Peters."

I grew hot with humiliation. "You...you invaded my privacy! You—"

"Please, don't be angry. I was afraid to tell you

before, but I had to do it, don't you see? I wanted to know about you. I *had* to know.''

I turned away from him, a stone in my heart. I rose, walked to the foot of the bed and leaned against the tall bedpost, clutching the round knob. So he knew. He had known all along that I had amnesia—the thing I was determined to hide, I suppose because it made me feel inferior. Other people knew who they were, had backgrounds and families. I stood alone. It was like being an outcast.

He came up in back of me, placing his hands on my shoulders, pressing them into my flesh. ''Please,'' he repeated, ''don't be angry. I'm glad to know. It helps me to share, to understand.''

The feel of him close to me, strong and protective, soothed me a little. Perhaps I was relieved that he knew.

''Did you tell anyone?'' I asked.

''Why should I tell anyone? But if Benjamin had lived. . . .''

I dropped my head over my hands. ''I feel so guilty,'' I said. ''I feel as though I killed him.''

''Don't say that!''

''But I do. You said yourself that if I left, it would kill him.''

Roughly he pulled me away from the bedpost, turning me to face him.

''For God's sake, don't say that. Your going away had nothing to do with it. Benjamin didn't die of another stroke. He was murdered—poisoned the night you left the house.''

I stood stunned for a moment. It was difficult for me to believe that this had happened, in this room! Shaking my head, I whispered incredulously, ''How. . . how do you know?''

He heaved a long sigh as though he was suddenly

weary. "I'll have to tell you. I'll have to tell you what happened after you left that night. But you look so tired—"

"I can't wait!" I cried. "Tell me now!"

"All right. But come back to Roma's room. Put on something comfortable while I get you a cup of tea. Then we'll talk."

And so in the early dawn, with the first streaks of light coming up over the edge of the ocean, I sat in one of the big white chairs, wrapped in a warm red velvet robe from Roma's closet, and drank the hot tea that André brought me. It steadied me, stopped the trembling that had begun to shake my body.

André sat on the hassock, facing me, just as he had that first morning when he had forced me into pretending to be Benjamin's granddaughter.

He began quietly, telling me how he had been hurrying home from Boston while I was running away on the bus. He had seen two doctors and made appointments, sure that they could help Benjamin. But he said he had an uneasy feeling that something was wrong, so he kept driving faster and faster, putting the gas pedal down to the floor. Still, it was dark when he arrived at the house, and he had hurried inside, running up the stairs two at a time on his way to my room, when Emma came rushing toward him.

"Mr. André come quickly—please—it's Mr. Benjamin! I think he's gone."

So André went to Benjamin, ordering Emma on the way to call the doctor. But when he entered the room, he saw at once that it was too late.

After Emma made the call she returned to explain, "I just left him for a little while. I had to go down and eat. And then, I was so tired... I peeked in and he seemed to be asleep. So I took a little nap, too—just about twenty minutes. And then when I came back .. ''

In her agitation she kept fussing. She straightened out Benjamin's covers and cleared up the little table near his bed.

"That cat," she fumed, "he comes in here and messes things up. Walks everywhere and knocks things over. I don't want the doctor to think—"

"Don't worry about anything, Emma. You were a wonderful help to him," André said, trying to soothe her.

But she was close to tears. "I had grown to love the old man. I thought he was going to make it."

By that time Clara and James, sensing some disturbance, had joined them. But André didn't take much notice of them. He was wondering where I was and hurried down the hall to Roma's room. The minute he opened the door, he said, he knew that I had left. There was an empty feeling about the room.

As he turned to leave, he confronted Clara and James, who had followed him, and he saw at once by their faces that they had found out about Roma—and me.

Of course, with Benjamin gone, he didn't have to mince words, so he demanded to know what they had said to me and where I had gone.

They pounced on him with a torrent of accusations. The three of them had a rousing fight right there on the threshold of Roma's room. The invectives flew in tones so loud that everybody in the house, so André said, knew that the real Roma was dead, that I had been a fraud impersonating her, and that he, André, was an accomplice in a crime.

Clara screamed shrilly that there would be an investigation. She had already called her lawyer and he would

call the police. She declared that she would never allow
me to escape, nor André, either. She and James would
see that we were brought to justice.

Only the arrival of the doctor subdued them. Still
fuming, they went back to their rooms. And André,
passing the open-mouthed Susan and Emma, led the
doctor to Benjamin's room.

After a brief examination, the doctor declared that
Benjamin had died of another stroke.

André quickly decided to tell him the whole truth
about Roma and me. With that in mind, he asked the
doctor to come back to Roma's room with him. But
first he wanted to call Benjamin's lawyer, who would at-
tend to the details of the funeral.

While André was speaking to the lawyer, the doctor
sat at the desk, making out the death certificate. It was
then that they both heard a strange retching sound coming from the dressing room.

As André hung up the phone, Satan crawled out. Before anyone could do anything for him, he shuddered,
convulsed and died.

"That cat," the doctor said, "was poisoned."

I jumped up, interrupting André's story.

"It was Clara!" I said. "She hated him. She wanted
to get rid of him."

He pulled me down again. "Sit still. Let me finish. Of
course I suspected her, but Satan wasn't likely to go
near her, nor James, either. Besides, all his food is in the
kitchen. So we went downstairs and questioned Susan
and Harry. They said the cat had not been down there
all day. But he often didn't come down till late. She had
his food out in a dish waiting."

So André took the dish, to have it examined.

And since he was going back to the hospital, the doctor agreed to take poor Satan to the laboratory to have

his stomach contents analyzed. He said he'd call André with the results.

And he did, about two hours later. The report was cyanide, dissolved in milk.

It was only a few minutes after the call that André, going back into Benjamin's room, had a terrible, almost unreasoning fear and called the doctor back.

"I would like," he said carefully, "to have Benjamin autopsied, too—just in case."

I sat straight up then, horrified. He took my hand and held it as he continued.

"Of course that was it. They found cyanide in his stomach. The doctor had to change the cause of death to poisoning. And he had to notify the police."

I burst out, "You were right! She is a scheming devil! Did you tell the police it was Clara? Did you?"

"No," he said, "but she tried to tell them it was you."

"Me!" I jumped up again, unable to control myself.

"She told them that you had run away that very night. She told them that you weren't Roma Starr at all, you were an imposter, and that you had surely given him the poisoned milk to get his money. And if Satan hadn't drunk it too, she insisted, you would have got away with it."

I stood very still, my blood frozen, as he went on, "Fortunately, they could see she was hysterical, and I was able to take them aside and assure them that you hadn't really run away. You would be back. As for the rest of the story, I figured I could explain it all to them later. They were very polite and patient, but of course I knew they would send out a call for you. Everybody has to be questioned. That was why I phoned Barnes in New York. Fortunately, he's an old friend, and I had a feeling you would go to New York—everybody does. I gave him your description and told him to find you fast and bring you back—that your grandfather was dead.''

I slowly bent my trembling knees and sank down on the edge of the chair again, staring straight ahead.

"Don't be frightened," he said, "I can explain. . . ." He must have seen how I looked, for he stopped in midsentence. Then he asked, "What's the matter?"

"André. . . ." My voice shook. "Did you say. . . poisoned. . .*milk*?"

"Yes. When they questioned Emma, she said she had seen the cat on Benjamin's table when she first walked in. He was lapping up some milk. There was a glass there, spilled over, half-empty. The cat ran, and she went for a towel to wipe up the mess. It was as she was finishing that she realized Benjamin was dead. Later, when she was clearing up the room before the doctor came, she had taken the glass away—put it in the bathroom but not washed it. Everything jibes; it was the milk, no question. But nobody admits to having brought him the milk. So everybody is under suspicion. There will have to be an inquest."

"I. . .gave it to him," I whispered. "It was I. I gave him the milk."

And I buried my face in my hands.

It was his turn to be shocked. He tore my hands from my face. "What are you saying? For God's sake—what are you saying!"

I told him about that afternoon. How, toward dusk, and when I was half-asleep, someone had come in and placed the milk on my table. How I had seen only a shadow of a figure leaving the room. And then, later, how I had taken it down to Benjamin.

He let out a long low breath. "That means," he said finally, "that the poison was meant for *you*."

We stared at each other, mutual fear in our eyes.

Then, abruptly, André collected himself. Still holding my hands he said, "Did anybody see you go down the hall? Did Emma know it was you who brought the milk?"

"No. Nobody saw me. But if you are thinking of my denying it, I won't. I've got to tell the truth. I'm through with deception."

"Of course, you're right, but don't say anything to anyone but Benjamin's lawyer, Mr. Hollester. Fortunately, he arrived yesterday, and he's taking care of everything, so he's staying here. I want you to see him first thing. Tell him just what happened."

Then, after a short pause, he said, "No, not first thing. Even before seeing him, before anything else, I want you to see Marie."

"Marie?"

"Yes. You remember I told you about Marie. She was Benjamin's housekeeper for more than thirty years and a second mother to Roma. They were very close. She's here now, down the hall. Just out of the hospital. It was an awful blow to her, Roma's death. She felt it as though Roma had been her own child. And then Benjamin's dying. She doesn't know yet that he was poisoned. She thinks, as we all did at first, that it was another stroke."

"Won't you have to tell her?"

"I'm leaving that to Mr. Hollester, later. First of all, I want you to go to her."

"But why?"

"She has something to tell you."

"About...Roma?"

He hesitated. Then he leaned down and kissed my brow, very gently.

"Go see her."

CHAPTER TWENTY

AFTER ANDRE LEFT, I threw off Roma's red robe and took a shower. All the while the words, "poisoned milk, poisoned milk," kept going through my mind. They sounded so sinister, not like something that happened in real life. Yet it had happened. Right here in this house.

I didn't want to believe that James would, or could, ever poison me. My mind rebelled. Yet, he *had* almost let me drown; he *had*, I was convinced, caused me to fall down the cellar stairs. Would it be different if he gave me poisoned milk? But the other two times were the result of spur-of-the-moment impulses; giving me the milk had to be premeditated, calculated. Was he capable of that? In my incredible naiveté, I could not believe it. And yet, Benjamin was dead. Benjamin, and poor Satan. I had to face it.

I saw myself in the mirror and realized my face had changed since I had last looked in this glass. It wasn't just the dark hair. No, it was something in my eyes, in the contour of my face. For the first time, I thought I saw in myself the look of a woman.

Quickly I combed my hair and put on a little lipstick. It looked stark against my white, drawn face, so I wiped most of it off. Then I stepped into my plain black dress. How sadly appropriate it was!

Well, I was ready now. I couldn't wait any longer. I would go to see Mr. Hollester. I had to talk to him, to tell him what I had done—and the sooner the better.

I opened the door and started down the stairs when I saw Susan coming out of the room next to Benjamin's with a tray in her hands.

"Good morning, ma'am," she said as she approached me. When she saw me looking at the empty tray, she explained, "It was for Marie. I'm glad she ate it all. She doesn't look very strong yet."

Marie! At the mention of her name, I suddenly remembered that André had said to go see her first thing. He seemed to think it was important.

Susan went on, "Do you want me to bring your breakfast up? Emma said perhaps you—"

"No, no, Susan. I don't want any breakfast. But tell me, is Marie sitting up? Is she able to talk, or do you think she's too ill?"

"Oh, she's not ill. She's up and dressed. It's just that she looks so frail since she's been in the hospital."

"I had better go in and see her."

"Oh, yes. I think that will be good for her. She's all broken up over Mr. Benjamin."

As Susan continued on, I turned around and went down the hall and knocked on Marie's door. The voice that said, "Come in," cracked a little. I turned the knob and entered.

I felt as though I had stepped back in time. The gleaming parquet floor was heavily waxed and polished, accented here and there with small multicolored hooked rugs. There was a four-poster bed, with a flowered canopy over it, and two dressers of highly polished mahogany. There was a fireplace, too, trim and unused, and by its side, a lovely old wooden cradle.

In a high-backed rocker next to the heavily curtained windows sat an old woman. Her thin hair was pulled back from her face, and her eyes were watery. I stood immobile for a second.

Then slowly she rose, and as she did, she stretched her arms out to me. The gesture went straight to my heart, and I ran to her; we hugged as though we were old friends. Suddenly she was weeping and mumbling, "Oh, Baby, my dear, my darling Baby."

Her sobs made me realize how shocking it must have been for her to see me, looking so much like Roma, with Roma so recently dead. I wanted to soothe her, to comfort her, but all I could think to do was pull a handkerchief from my pocket and try to help her dry her tears.

"Come, Marie," I said at last, "sit down. You're not well yet. You must sit down."

She sank into the rocker again, and I sat on the floor beside her, looking up into her thin drawn face. Finally she made an effort to control herself. She wiped her eyes and, shaking her head a little as she gazed down at me, said in a voice choked with emotion, "Baby, don't you know me?"

Prickles of confusion, almost like fear, surged through me. What did she mean, "Don't you know me?" I knew she was Marie, Benjamin's housekeeper.

Then she reached out her hand and passed it over my brow, just as Roma had done that night at the hospital. She stopped when she touched the scar hidden under my bangs.

"It's...still there," she whispered. "The scar is still there."

I sat very quietly. In that moment something deep reached me. I seemed, vaguely, to be remembering something. Just a little thing: I remembered a hand dressing a wound, long, long ago. Whose hand?

Marie was still looking at me with her pale, red-rimmed eyes. She cupped my face in her hands and said, "No, I see you don't remember me. Mr. André told me you wouldn't. He told me you had that sickness, that amnesia. He said you didn't even remember that you were Roma's baby sister. But you are, my dear, you are.''

I think my breath stopped. I think the world stopped. Nothing moved, not even an eyelid. I remained as I was, staring up at her.

She went on, ''You look just like her. You always did, except for your dark hair—dark like your mother's. I think that's why she always favored you.''

She stroked my hair, weeping a little. And I, who had wept so much in the past over my lost identity, was dry-eyed and silent now...in shock. Was it possible? I was being told who I was. *Who I was!*

She pulled me to her then, so that I felt her soft body against mine. My head whirled dizzily. Still leaning against Marie, I seemed to be running down a flight of stairs, then suddenly tumbling wildly head over heels and falling, falling—and hitting something hard. Then blood was streaming down on my face, and a voice was crying, ''She's cracked her head! Baby's cracked her head! Get the doctor!''

I suddenly clutched Marie's hand and looked up, as though awakening from a dream, awakening to a revelation.

''My scar! Those stairs! It was here! In this house!'' I sat trembling while Marie went on.

''Yes, my dear—you were only three years old. I held you while your mother called the doctor and he stitched it up. He said it could have killed you, it was so deep. But he said if we massaged it, later when it healed, the scar might not show. But—'' She broke down and her voice tightened in her throat. ''But we never did get it massaged for you. Your mother took you away, the bandage still on your head.''

''Took me...away?''

"Yes. God knows where. It was on a hot summer day. We were going down to the beach for a clambake, and your mother said that you shouldn't go, not with your wounded head. I offered to stay, but she said no, she would. And then, when we came back, you were both gone."

As she spoke a shadowy scene came to me: a dark-haired woman was hurrying about, putting a hat on me when I didn't want a hat on. She lifted me up in one arm, and clutched a heavy suitcase in the other. Then the two of us rushed noiselessly through the empty house, out a side door into a waiting car. A strange man was sitting at the wheel, and the car's motor was running...and that was all. Imagination...or memory? I couldn't tell.

Marie, oblivious to what had been going on in my mind, was still talking, pouring out her story.

"We never found out where you went that day. Never. Your father and grandfather had detectives searching, but finally they gave up. They thought she had left the country with that English actor—one of the leading men in the summer theater they had here. She was a beautiful woman, your mother, but—well—frivolous, and I guess more lighthearted than the folks here in Maine. I guess she didn't really belong here. She had been a ballet dancer, you know, born in France. And well, anyway, we never saw her, or you, again."

She stopped. I was coming out of shock a little. My blood beginning to flow, my heart to pump. Now that I had been told, it seemed as though I had known it all along—for of course I had been carrying around, deep in my subconscious, the knowledge that I belonged here. Elation was rising in me. But at the same time, fluttering through my whole body, was a kind of panic.

Marie had said, "We never found out where you

went. We never saw you or your mother again.'' Well, *I* didn't know where we went that day either. The rest of my life was a blank—my whole life!

Suddenly frantic, I cried, ''Help me! Help me, Marie! I can't remember!''

But Marie couldn't help me. ''That's all I know, child. You were taken away. You were only three.''

Then, trying to soothe me, she said, ''But I can tell you what happened here after you and your mother left. It was all very sad. After they had given up searching, when they realized there was no hope, your father became morose. He started to brood and to drink. But your grandfather soon put a stop to that. He said we had to forget and pretend to be happy—for Roma's sake. He thought if we ceased to speak of you and your mother, Roma would forget. So he imposed a silence. We were forbidden to mention anything among ourselves or to anyone else. All signs of you and your mother were removed. And after a while things settled down and it seemed that Roma had forgotten.

''But she hadn't. She said to me once, months afterward, 'Where do you think my mother and sister are? Do you think they will ever come back?' Of course I didn't know, and I was afraid to discuss it with her. Another time, out of the blue, she said to me, 'I wonder if it healed.' 'If what healed?' I asked. 'My sister's cut— on her head.'

''I told her, of course it had healed and to forget about it. I told her that was what her father and her grandfather wanted, and if she loved them, she would forget. After that she never spoke to me about it.

''But it was a strange thing—everybody thinking and remembering, but no one ever mentioning it. Everyone pretending.

''We were all glad when finally, after seven years,

your father got a divorce, the kind you can get when someone deserts you, and he married Miss Clara. She wasn't as pretty or as gay as your mother, but she brought James with her, and it made it pleasant for Roma. By that time she was twelve and he was fourteen. They became great companions. Well, more than that, I guess.

"It was after that that Roma seemed to change. She grew...well, a little wild. She had always been strong-willed and reckless, but James and she, they were a pair. They were inseparable, but they fought—oh, how they fought! And then they'd make up. We all thought they would marry, and we figured it would be pretty stormy.

"But he went off to college and then to war. And then one day Mr. André came along, and before we knew it he and Roma ran off and got married."

Here she stopped, worn out from the emotion of reliving it all. I sat silently, too, leaning my head against her knees. I couldn't move or speak. To me, nothing seemed real.

Finally she spoke again, her soft voice cracking a little. "You mustn't think that any of us forgot you. You were always there, like a presence in the house, though no one spoke of you after Mr. Benjamin forbade it. And you mustn't blame him. Mr. Benjamin was a good man. He thought he was doing what was best for Roma. I know once, it was about 1941 or '42, we received two letters. I knew they were from Mrs. Starr—from Roma's mother. After all those years she had finally written. But it was too late. Your father had died and Roma was grown. I gave them to Mr. Benjamin, but I know he never told Roma. I don't think he ever opened them. It was hard for him to forgive."

At that she shook her head and began to cry softly

again. I suppose she was remembering him, grieving for him.

To give her a little time, I got up and went to her dressing room and brought her a glass of water. She drank it gratefully and handed the glass back to me. Just as I reached for it, I remembered my ring. My satyr ring. The pain, the joy, of my life.

I held my hand up in front of her. "Marie, tell me, do you know this ring? Have you seen it before? Did it belong to my mother? My father? Somebody here?"

She looked at the ring and gave a little gasp. It frightened her, I could tell, for she pulled back. Then, to my great disappointment, she began to shake her head.

"Oh, no, my dear, I've never seen such a thing. Your mother never had anything like that. She always liked beautiful, dainty things. This is—" she searched for a world "—grotesque!"

I felt hurt and pulled back my hand.

"Are you sure?"

"I'm sure. I've never seen it. I would remember a thing like that. It doesn't belong here." And then, with a shudder, she asked, "Wherever did you get a thing like that?"

"I don't know," I whispered, "I don't know."

A dark shadow closed slowly over me. Was my ring, then, to remain a mystery to me...forever?

CHAPTER TWENTY-ONE

IT WAS ONLY A MOMENT LATER that Susan knocked on the door and stepped inside.

"Excuse me," she said and paused just long enough to show that she saw we had been through an emotional scene.

"Excuse me," she said again, "but Mr. Hollester sent me up. He wants to see you, Marie. Right away. He says he has been called to town and can't wait any longer."

Marie rose, a little shakily, and smoothed out her dress. "I'll come right down."

I rose too. "I had better come with you."

"No, dear, you don't need to. I know my way well enough after all these years. You'll want a little time to yourself now, I'm sure. But wait here for me. There's so much more we have to say to each other." And she left with Susan.

I sank slowly into the rocker Marie had been sitting in. I did, indeed, need some time to digest what I had heard.

My mind flew back to my meeting with Roma in the hospital. Roma—my sister! That lovely, pale, far-off girl staring at me from her bed. Had she known?

I remembered feeling drawn to her, feeling close to her from the very beginning. Had she felt the same pull? Had she divined who I was when she asked me to go to her grandfather? Or was it when she touched my brow and felt my scar?

Why didn't she tell me? Of course, I had told her I was Sara Smith. That must have puzzled her. And she was weak; she was dying. She didn't have the strength to talk very much—just a few words. I tried to remember what she had said. Everything would mean something to me now. Every word would be significant.

And then it came to me. The very first time she looked at me, her very first word had been *baby*. She had called out to me, "Baby!"

And I'd thought she had a baby somewhere. But no. She had been calling *me*. She had known right away.

And then it struck me with an incredible stab that I still didn't know my name, my real given name! Marie had called me Baby, just as Roma had. Surely that was just a nickname. How could I have let Marie go without telling me? I could barely wait for her to come back. Restless, I jumped up and began to pace the floor.

All at once, I remembered the letters, the letters Benjamin had asked me to get for him. They must be the ones Marie had spoken of!

I rushed to the door and in two minutes I had run down those fearful, wobbly stairs and begun searching for the key to the bin. With trembling fingers I found it and opened the bin and then the trunk. And there on a shelf all by itself was a box. Even before I opened it, I knew the letters were in there. And I was right. Each was in a faded envelope, unopened, and postmarked London, 1941. One was addressed to Mr. Edward Starr, the other to Miss Roma Starr. Neither had a return address.

I was awed. I sat down on the trunk in the storage bin, and in the dim light of the bulb overhead, I opened the letter to Mr. Edward Starr. I paused, concerned about invading his privacy. And yet—who but I should be reading them? I was the last link between these two suffering people: my mother, my father.

Slowly I unfolded the paper.

Dear Edward,

The guns of war are booming over here, and the world seems to be shaking. Perhaps that is why at last I have the courage to write to you. This will not be long. I don't intend to worry you—I have caused too much of that, I'm sure. I only want to say that I am sorry for the pain I must have given you. I couldn't write before because I was afraid you would come after me. I hope you have married again and that you are happy. I know you won't understand, but I had to try to live a freer life than the one you good people live up there on the coast of Maine. I suppose I am a coward and did it all wrong. It is getting late now, late for everything, even for forgiveness. But I want you to know that your baby daughter is well and thriving, and that one day soon I will tell her she must go to see her father—her real father—and her grandfather. She is a good, beautiful young lady, and you will be proud of her.

Again, forgive me—if you can.

There was a signature, but it was scrawled so loosely that I couldn't make it out. As in a dream, I picked up the other letter and, between tears, read:

Dearest Roma,

Perhaps by now you have forgotten your mother, and perhaps that is what I deserve. But my heart has ached for you for almost fifteen years, and now I must ask your forgiveness. Now that you

are grown, it is possible that you might understand.
I could not go on living in the house that is your
home. It was never mine. I was an alien soul there,
starving for a free life. And one day I couldn't bear
it any longer and took a drastic step. I want to explain: I took your baby sister because I felt she was
too young to leave behind. And also I felt you were
more likely to thrive in that atmosphere, for you
were a great favorite of your father and grandfather. In a way, I sacrificed you for them. I had to
leave them someone to love, don't you see? They
are good people—I always knew that—only so different from me, so unbending. I was dying—I
mean, my soul was shriveling up, and I was still
young then and I had to run.

Try to understand, and if you can—forgive.

Your tearful, loving
Mother

As I folded the yellowing papers, I sat stilled, subdued. All that suffering. My mother, my father, my
dear Benjamin and Roma. And I had not known any of
it. Even before I lost my memory, my mother had not
told me—or had she, later?

Slowly the agony of not remembering—not even
now—was beginning to take hold of me. I sat there,
struggling with myself, when I was abruptly brought
back to the present by noise overhead. I heard someone
running, and people talking in loud voices. Quickly I
replaced the letters in the box, closed the trunk, and
hurried upstairs. As I opened the cellar door, I saw
Emma running from the library and rushed to her.

"It's Marie," she told me as she continued up the
stairs. "She's fainted. I have some smelling salts up
here...."

I turned and saw Clara and James and a strange man hurrying from the dining room toward the open door of the library. Even from a fleeting glance, I could see they looked different.

James was drawn and solemn, all his élan gone. Clara, dressed in a defiant red sweater, was flushed, tense. They crowded in the doorway, followed by the man. I supposed he was their lawyer.

I hurried right past them to Marie. She was stretched out on one of the brown leather couches. Another strange man was standing over her. When he saw me, he said, "I'm Mr. Hollester, your grandfather's attorney."

I lost no time in kneeling beside Marie and making an effort to bring her to. I took her head in my hands and held it down over the side of the couch to bring the blood to it.

"I tried to break it to her gently," Mr. Hollester was saying, "about how Benjamin died, but she just couldn't take the shock. She just fainted dead away. I barely had time to catch her."

By now Emma was back. "Let her smell this," she said as she knelt beside me and held the smelling salts under Marie's nose. "I've told Susan to make some strong tea."

Marie began coming to. She fluttered her eyelids. Then she began to mumble, "Oh, no, *no*. It was my fault. I should have told someone. I should have told someone!"

Susan came in then with the tea and, following her, towering above everyone, was André. He dominated the room as soon as he walked in, and everyone stepped aside to let him by. Emma and I rose at the same time, making room. As he sat down beside Marie, she seemed to gain strength from his closeness. She sat up and leaned against him.

He took the tea from Susan. "Here," he said, his voice soothing, tender, "drink this. It will be good for you."

Obediently she drank, but she couldn't stop crying. Between gulps she gasped a little, trying to say something.

"Don't try to talk," André said, "it's been a shock to you. Just drink some of your tea."

"You don't understand," she said weakly, persistently. "It was my fault."

"Of course it wasn't your fault. There's nothing you could have done. Just try to rest now. Don't cry."

But her sobbing grew louder, the pain contorting her face. "I could have saved him if I had been here. Because I knew...I knew!"

At her last words we all unconsciously inched closer to her, even Mr. Hollester, who leaned over her.

"Marie, what did you know?"

She looked up. "I...I...." Then she was overcome with weeping again, and André took out his handkerchief and handed it to her.

"I knew he was going to do it," she said at last. Then turning to André, she added, "I should have warned you."

Mr. Hollester put his hand firmly on her shoulder and spoke in his lawyer's voice, the voice of authority.

"Please. Try to control yourself, Marie. Tell us what you are trying to say."

She responded at once, more calmly. "Why, just that I knew he would try to kill himself."

"But he couldn't have killed himself. He was paralyzed." It was Clara who spoke. Her voice was still shrill but a little shaky. She glanced at me with hostility as she added, "Someone else must have poisoned him."

"That's true," Mr. Hollester acknowledged, backing

her up. "You know Mr. Benjamin was paralyzed, Marie. I don't think he could have killed himself. He was helpless."

"That's just it, don't you see? That's what he feared, being helpless. He swore, he told me over and over that if he ever became helpless, he didn't want to live. He had a small stroke, a year ago, and he recovered. But he was haunted by it. He said he didn't want to lie around being a burden to everyone. He said he would do something about it."

"But where could he have got the poison? He couldn't move," André said.

"I think I know," Marie said, "I think I know." And she was about to start crying again when André put the teacup on the floor and took her hands in his.

"Marie, don't cry anymore. This is very important to all of us. Try to just tell us what you think happened."

"I think he killed himself," she answered promptly, "and it was my fault. I knew he had some pills, some capsules. I saw him hiding them one day, a long time ago, after he had recovered from his other stroke. I thought it was peculiar—the way he acted—guilty, like. I knew they were something he shouldn't have or he wouldn't be hiding them. They were in his hand, six maybe."

"But Marie, even if he had them hidden, he couldn't have got to them himself. Benjamin couldn't get out of bed."

"He wouldn't have had to get out of bed. All he needed to do was reach up. Once he could move his arms, he could easily have got them."

"Where? Where did he have them?"

"In his bedpost. The knobs in the headboard—they unscrew. I meant to take the pills away, but at first I was afraid to touch them—Mr. Benjamin had a terrible temper—and then, after a while...oh, God forgive me, I forgot.''

I didn't wait to hear anymore. I turned and ran out of the room and up the stairs. I could hear a commotion in back of me. They were following me. I didn't care. Nothing mattered now but to find those pills—if there were any still there.

By the time I had the knob of that old mahogany bedpost unscrewed, they were all around me—Clara and James and André and Marie, even Susan and Emma. Mr. Hollester came up alongside me, looking, I suppose, for evidence.

And there it was: a single capsule, wedged deep in the empty well of the bedpost.

"I'll take that," Mr. Hollester said, a kind of elation in his voice. "It could prove suicide if it matches what was in his stomach. We'll see." And he took a handkerchief and wrapped the pill in it.

At this, Marie cried out, "Oh, Mr. Benjamin, why did you do it? Why did you do it!"

And then she began crying hysterically. André put his arm around her and quickly led her away.

As they left the room, Emma clicked her tongue. "Six. She said there were six capsules. He must have taken five—no wonder he died."

"But he was paralyzed," Clara's voice broke in, queer and strained. "How could he...?"

"No, he couldn't have swallowed them." Emma was figuring it out. "But he could have dropped them in the milk to dissolve. He could move his arms quite well near the end. He could have reached up and got them and dropped them in."

I was still standing there, frozen, the wooden knob of the bedpost in my hand. Then I heard myself saying, "It was my fault. I brought him the milk. I only wanted to help him. But I helped to kill him."

It was Aunt Clara, of all people, who tried to comfort me. She came over beside me and said her first kind words to me.

"Don't blame yourself, child. You did what you thought was right. And he did what he thought was right. That's the best any of us can do."

What she said was true, I suppose, but I was beyond consoling. I was—had been for so many days—struggling with too many emotions. And now they all seemed to come together as in a volcano about to erupt. There was only one thing I could think to do—run.

I dashed from the room and down the stairs without waiting to put on a wrap. I ran out the door and into the fresh air and down the narrow steps from the cliff to the ocean. Then, still unthinking, not knowing anything but that I had to run, to find release, I raced along the shore edge, careless of the spume or the damp sand, stumbling occasionally over shells and rocks but going on and on, gasping as I went.

I came at last to a barrier. The shore curved, leaving a rocky cliff before me. Undaunted, I started to scramble up—clutching the rocks and brush, slipping and starting over, until finally I reached the top: a long flat rocky ledge jutting out to sea.

On this I fell, exhausted. I felt the cold, damp rock against my cheek and clutched its rough surface with my fingers. I lay there gasping, panting.

Only then did I realize there was a rage inside me that all my running could not subdue, rage at the world. I had been told I had a family, and just as I had been about to touch them, first Roma and then Benjamin, they had been snatched away. Now there was nothing to cling to, no one to help me make it real.

Even more terrible was my rage at myself. For now

that I had been told I had a family, now that I had been told *who* I was, I still could not remember. My mind was still a blank. I remembered nothing but a vague incident involving me as a child of three. Would nothing wake me, ever?

In my rage I lifted up my fists to beat the rock—and there on my hand was my ring, glittering and triumphant. That same old impudent face was staring up at me, taunting me, gloating over the fact that I still could remember nothing.

"You," I screamed at it, "you are a fraud! And a demon. You have nothing to do with my family—you don't even belong here! You have tortured me long enough!"

And I pulled at the licentious green face and tore the ring off my finger. Then, just as thunder began to roll in the distance, I threw it with all my might out toward the sea.

Held back by the strong winds, it fell into a crack an inch from the edge of the ledge. I wished it had gone over. I was through with it, through suffering over it.

I laid my head down, closed my eyes, and listened to the thunder. Let there be rain and thunder and lightning! Let the storm come and carry me away!

But what came, after a little while, was André. And when I heard his step and felt him kneel down beside me and put his arms around me, I knew it was he I wanted. I knew that he could heal all my wounds—if only he would. If only he would love me as he had loved his Sybil, nothing else would matter.

He was busy wrapping a coat around me.

"What are you doing out here? You'll die of the cold."

I was shivering, it was true. The coat felt good.

"Come, we must get back to the house. There's a terrible storm coming."

"I like it here," I said perversely, resisting his pull.

"What's the matter with you?" He shook me lightly by the shoulders. "I thought you would be happy. Didn't you talk to Marie? Didn't she tell you?"

"Yes, she told me."

"Well, then. . . ." He seemed incredulous. "Doesn't it change things? Doesn't it help you to know that you are actually Benjamin's granddaughter?"

I looked up at him, a question forming. "André, did you know? Did you know all the time?"

"Well, I. . ." he said, hesitating, hugging me to him before completing his answer, "I did know but—"

I pushed him away from me, appalled. "Why didn't you tell me? How could you let me suffer like that?"

"Don't be angry! Of course I wanted to tell you, but I was following the doctor's instructions. I told you I called London and spoke to Dr. Peters. He said to hold back, to give you a chance to remember things by yourself."

"But I didn't—I didn't remember anything!"

"He said it wouldn't help to tell you. Even the doctors I spoke to when I went to Boston said there would be no point in telling you. It would only confuse you. But we hoped when you saw Marie in the room where you were born and she talked to you that you would remember it all. And if you didn't, I told her to tell you anyhow. I couldn't stand it any longer."

"Yes, she told me," I cried, "she told me and still I don't remember." I gave up then and wept against his shoulder.

He waited, patting my head, trying to soothe me. Then after a while, he said, "Can't you see it was better this way? Not even knowing he was your grandfather, you came to love Benjamin Starr. Sara Smith came to love Benjamin Starr for himself. Just as Sara Smith came to love me. You do love me, don't you?''

"Yes, you know I do."

"Then does it matter that you can't remember?"

"Not . . . so much.''

"That's what I wanted to hear—that it won't matter, not remembering, as long as we love each other."

Then he folded me in his arms and gave me what I needed—what I had needed all along: the deep warm comfort of his love. There on the rocky ledge, with the storm clouds gathering and the distant lightning coming closer, we knew we loved each other.

I touched his face and looked into his eyes. I wanted to be certain of him.

"André . . . do you, really? Do you love me . . . the way you loved Sybil?"

He didn't hesitate. He looked back into my eyes as though he were swearing a pact. "I do," he said solemnly. "I love you the way I loved Sybil."

"She won't come between us? She won't make us unhappy?"

"I don't think so," he said, "I really don't think so—not anymore. Not now that I know you love me the way she used to."

It was sweet music. A peace came over me. It didn't matter that the skies were about to open up and deluge us.

But André stirred. "Come, we've got to get out of here now. It's dangerous. We could be struck by lightning."

I let him grasp my hands and pull me up. He tucked me into his coat.

"Hurry!" he said. "We've got to get to shelter. There's a cove a little way up the shore, under the cliff. We'll wait there till it passes."

And he began to lead the way down the side of the cliff I had so painfully climbed. Once down, he took my hand as we began to run close to the overhanging cliff, away from the already angry ocean. As we ran, the thunder rolling overhead, the forks of lightning coming closer, it seemed that I had run this way with him before. It was a wild thought, matching the day.

We stumbled on, our hands linked, until I suddenly remembered my ring. I stopped, pulling him up short, and cried out, "My ring! I've got to go back for my ring!"

I can still see his face turned toward me, as white as the crested waves. He didn't let go of my hand, and I yanked at it, trying to free myself.

"I've got to go! I've got to get it!"

"Where, in God's name—where is it?"

"On the ledge!"

"On the ledge?"

"Yes. It's on the ledge. I meant to throw it into the sea, but it didn't go over. It's there, stuck in a crack. And now I want it back. I've got to go—let me go—let me go!"

He grabbed me, and for some inexplicable reason kissed me fiercely, as the first giant drops of rain began to fall. Then he released me and said, "I'll go. I'll get our talisman. You run on to the cove. I'll find it."

And he went. "It's on the edge!" I called after him "Be careful!"

I watched him for a moment, and then I turned and started for the cove. The thunder was growing louder, crackling like canon fire, and I was a little frightened. I knew I shouldn't have let him go, and yet, I had a terrible, inexpressible sense of loss about my ring. A wave of loneliness had come over me when I felt my empty finger. A wave of guilt, a sense of betrayal, for having tossed it away.

And then, as I began to run, I realized that he had said "our" talisman. What did he mean? The ring was *mine*. My secret, my pain, my past.

I think I was only a few yards away from the little shelter when the lightning struck. It passed me by a few feet, but the shock went through me, convulsing me. I saw it streak by; I felt its deadly pull, and in an instant I was thrown flat on the ground. I hit hard, as though tossed by a great force, and as I blacked out, I heard the crackling of a tree and saw the flash of flame.

I suppose it was only a few minutes before I opened my eyes again. The struck tree had fallen down from the cliff and was burning only a few feet from me, the bright flame daring the rains to quench it. I could feel its warmth. But I couldn't move.

Something had happened to me. Something so profound, I couldn't move even a little finger.

CHAPTER TWENTY-TWO

Everything is changed. I lie very still, feeling the wet sand against my cheek, the rain like a flood pouring over me. All at once I am aware, as other people are, of my whole life. It has come back just the way the doctors said it would—from the beginning. I am restored unto myself.

I lie quietly under the deluge, reliving the past years in a few seconds. It is not exactly remembering. Rather, it is "knowing." I "know" the little girl who was carried off, away from this coast and her other family members, her sister and her father and grandfather, even Marie. I "know" the confusion of traveling with my mother and a strange man whom she tells me now to call father.

I know, a little more clearly, the years of moving. Trains, buses, planes, boats; cities, countries, hotels, houses, cottages. It is a gypsy life, happy, in its way.

My new father and my mother (whom I now recognize as the woman whose portrait I had found in the closet) are bright and happy and carefree. I see him perform on a stage many times—too many—in different places.

For a while there is no real home. But finally we begin to settle down, to stay longer in one place. In England—London. I am growing up. I am fifteen when the shadow of the war falls upon us. My "father" tries to do his part, though he is not very young anymore and, so my mother says, not very fit. One night he goes out in a boat to Dunkirk to try to bring some soldiers back. And he does not return.

My mother despairs and weeps. She crumbles. She changes from a carefree, lighthearted person to a timid frightened one. She becomes terrified, clinging to me, wanting me close to her all the time. I try to fill her needs. In a sense, I become her mother.

But by the time I am seventeen, I know I must do my part. I lie about my age and become an ambulance driver. I see and experience the horrors of war. I work all through the night, never sleeping before dawn. I see buildings collapsing, bodies strewn about. I help to put them on the stretchers, sometimes help to dig them out while the fires rage. And always there is the terrible noise in my ears, in my bones, shrieking at me, shaking me.

But I am young and strong. I do not break until one morning when I come home I find my little dog dead. Not bombed; just dead from the noise, the fright. He had crawled under my bed during a bombing and just died. It was too much for him. It is too much for me, too. His death unnerves me like nothing else. I break down.

They tell me to take some time off, a few weeks to rest. I walk through a little park, aimlessly, guilt in my soul for not carrying on, for not being able to carry on. I stop beside a young man in an RAF uniform who is sitting on a bench with a pad propped against his knees. He is doing a sketch with watercolor pencils and trying to use his own spit for water. He is wearing dark glasses that look like flying goggles.

He looks up angrily and yells, "Hey, you! Miss! Do you mind moving? You're blocking my view."

I move, but I am annoyed. I walk over and stand be-

hind him, looking over his shoulder. He slashes away at the scene furiously, ruining it. I know I am bothering him. Finally I begin to laugh. I can't help myself. Such temperament! I have never encountered such a temper!

"You're spoiling it," I venture.

"You spoiled it!" he snaps. "You got in the way of my view."

"I'm not there now. It's your goggles. You could see better if you took them off."

He yanks them off and looks at me. I see a pair of flashing blue eyes. We stop quarreling—and fall in love. After a few minutes I say shyly, "Why don't you go on with your painting?"

"No. No... I'm not really any good at scenes." And he starts to cover his pad and put his pencils away.

"What are you good at?"

"Portraits," he says without modesty. "I'm very good at portraits." Then suddenly he asks, "Would you like me to do your portrait?"

I sit down on the bench beside him. "Perhaps, some day."

We talk till evening. I discover that he had been studying art in Paris when the war broke out and had crossed the Channel immediately to join the RAF. I find him heroic and charming—a little mysterious, even a little poetic. He talks of "the gods" and "fate" and "destiny"—and satyrs.

I am intrigued with him and with the ring he has on his little finger. It is an enormous thing with a lifelike face carved into the huge emerald stone. Its devilish head is thrown back in raucous laughter, and it has two tiny horns in place of ears. It both attracts me and frightens me. When he holds it up for me to see, I jump back as though it could bite.

"Why do you wear a thing like that? It's alive!"

"Of course it's alive. He's Silenus, my satyr."

"Your what?"

"My satyr. A satyr is a Greek demigod. Satyrs are gods of pleasure and abandonment. This one's name is Silenus. He's my talisman."

"What do you mean by that?"

"He guards me. He watches over me."

"Do you believe that?"

"Of course. You have to have something to believe in—up there. Something to hold on to. A good luck piece, you know."

"But he looks so. . . wild!"

"He is wild. Wild with pleasure. That's what he believes in. Be happy! He doesn't believe in all this suffering going on."

"This is no time to enjoy," I say primly. *"We have duties."*

"Duties! Duties!" he mimics. *"Just the same, I have a feeling you are going to have to answer his call one day—with me."*

I shiver a little, in a thrilling way. I know I will answer, one day. . .

Now, here on the beach in Maine, I am lying quite still—experiencing, absorbing the new-old past. This scene has grown vivid with life, standing out from the rest. It is so vivid that I am forced to move. I raise my head and the present breaks through. I hear, not just the thunder still rolling, the rains still pouring over me, but a voice.

I hear André calling from a distance.

"Sybil! Sybil!"

For the first time I know he means me. Not somebody else, not a ghost, but me. Me! I am his Sybil!

I hear his running steps thudding against the sand. He reaches me. He falls down beside me, frantic.

"Good God, what happened to you? I saw you fall. You haven't been hit, have you? That tree? The lightning?"

I see his face clearly in the dying sparks of the tree. André! André! I want to say, "Everything is all right now. You mustn't be angry anymore. I have come back. The gods—they didn't really destroy us. We haven't lost each other."

But I cannot speak. Not yet.

He lifts me and carries me a little way to the cove. He puts me down and feels my face, my hands.

"Are you all right?"

I manage a single word: "Yes."

"Then I must go back. I still have to find the ring."

"No!" I cry out. "Don't go. I don't need my ring anymore."

He wrenches himself away from me, shocked. "Of course you do! I must get it."

And he is gone before I can stop him, before I can tell him. I watch him running along the shore, as I have watched him before. . . somewhere, sometime.

And then I remember, moment for moment, the last scene of all.

We are on another shore, in another storm. It is Cornwall, England. Cornwall by the sea—as wild and rocky as this coastline here in Maine.

We are young and in love, and we have fled the horrors of London. André has three days before he has to leave for God knows where. And we have fled the shattering bombs, the gaping holes and crumbling roofless buildings, the grim-faced people—even my clinging mother, who wants me at home. We have hitched a ride in a buddy's plane and landed here at Cornwall, away from the smell of death.

We are happy as children should be happy, carefree

as satyrs. We make a pact down by the sea, a foolish pact, to be happy even if the whole world should perish.

For three days we run and play on the empty beach. We make love in a cove like this one, with the sound of the breakers pounding in our ears.

On the last evening we spread out a blanket on the rocky beach and talk secretly, deliciously, of the future. André looks different in the dark, under the stars. He laughs, throwing his head back in wild abandon, like the face on his ring, his satyr. I don't mind. I, too, am learning to enjoy myself.

But when the moon rises, white and brilliant, lighting up the sky, we remember. We have to remember.

There will be bombs dropping on London, on Bristol and Cardiff, on Exeter and Devon. There will be death and destruction.

We gaze solemnly at each other in the white moonlight. There is no escape. Tomorrow we will be part of it again.

Suddenly he pulls off his ring and shows me that he has had the inner band engraved with my initials, two exotic snakes that form a double "S"—for Sybil Starr.

"But why? It is your ring."

"I want you to have it."

"But I can't take it. It's your talisman."

"It's your talisman, too, now."

"But you need it to keep you safe. Your good luck piece. You said so."

"I want to leave it with you. Silenus has been through the war with me—through the Battle of Britain and more. He's part of me. I want to leave a part of me with you."

He takes my hand and slips the ring onto my finger.

"Now," he says, "he will guard you as I would if I could. But I warn you—" he wags his finger at me "—if *you ever take it off, Silenus will haunt you. If you forget me, he will give you no peace."*

"How could I ever forget you?"

"I don't think you could. But—" his voice suddenly sinks "—I have a terrible fear."

"A fear? Of what?"

"Of losing you."

Here he presses me to him as if to prevent it.

"But why? Don't you trust me? Don't you know I love you?"

"Of course. It's not that. It's something else. I think it's because...." He nestles his face in my hair and whispers, "I think it's because I'm too happy."

I look up at him, incredulous. "Afraid? Because you're too happy?"

"Yes. Haven't you ever heard that if you are too happy, the gods will be jealous and destroy you?"

"But that's only superstition!" I pull away and shake him a little. "You mustn't believe that! It isn't true."

But even as I say it, I feel fear inching its way through my body. Suppose it is true?

He bends his head and kisses my fingers, kisses my ring, our ring. Then he looks up into my eyes.

"Never lose it and we won't lose each other."

"I'll never take it off," I promise. "I'll never lose it."

And we cling together, there on the lonely beach in the white moonlight, with the tide pushing the wild breakers closer and closer....

How could I have forgotten, I ask myself now, accusingly. How could I have forgotten?

And immediately, as though in answer to my question, another scene follows:

It is the same night. Later. Clouds have hidden the moon. It is dark and the storm comes, unbelievably wild.

We are glad because we know it will stop the bombs. We run out, arms flung up, and embrace the torrential rains. Drenched, we dance on the beach and hug and weep. We are no longer afraid to be too happy. All will be well.

In the morning we hitch a ride back to London again. Reality. Ugliness. Destruction.

I go with him to his post, just in time for him to take off. Clutching his ring, I try to remember that I have a part of him here on my finger.

"Never lose it and we won't lose each other."

I watch him disappear from my sight.

Forever?

Once he's gone, I remember my mother for the first time in days.

I hurry home, running all the way. But when I arrive at what should have been my home, there is nothing but roofless walls, piles of broken stones. I stand there staring at what has been a direct hit.

Panic sets in. My guilt swells as I begin to run through the rubble. Mother! Mother! Where are you?

But she is nowhere. Gone. Gone while I played at the ocean's edge. While I was too happy.

I begin to run. I run and run and run, calling, "Where are you, where are you?" I keep running and calling. I cannot stop.

Somewhere along the way I remember André. He will help me. I need you, André. Where are you? Where are you?

But he too is gone. I keep running.

Then suddenly, incredibly, the sky is full of bombers again, shrieking the terrible noise of the buzz bombs.

Everything is exploding. I am thrown to the ground. The bombs rain down around me. At last I let go. . . of everything.

When I awaken in the hospital, all is quiet. All is. . blank. Only the ring on my finger, my satyr, remembers.

Now, here in a cove on the cold coast of Maine, I was awake again, awake as I had not been since that night on the coast of Cornwall.

I sprang up and rushed from the shelter out into the rain, crying, "Where are you? Where are you?" as I had done so many times in my nightmares.

Only this time I was not dreaming. I knew whom I was calling. I knew where he was. I saw him far up the shore climbing down from the ledge.

He waved his arm and I knew he had found my ring, our ring—our talisman.

I raced, toward him then, arms outstretched. And we met—once again under a thunderous sky, drenched with rain and tears.

Everything is over. Everything is beginning.